Patricia O'Connor

THE SEARCH FOR JACQUELINE

PublishAmerica
Baltimore

First printing

At the specific preference of the author, PublishAmerica allowed this work to remain exactly as the author intended, verbatim, without editorial input.

Cover Photograph by Wood Koizumi

Photograph on back cover by Mark Brennan

This is a work of fiction. Names, characters, corporations, institutions, organizations, events or locales in this novel are either the product of the author's imagination or, if real, used fictitiously. Any resemblance to actual persons (living or dead) is entirely coincidental.

ISBN: 1-4241-5568-1 (softcover)
ISBN: 978-1-4489-9239-3 (hardcover)
PUBLISHED BY PUBLISHAMERICA, LLLP
www.publishamerica.com
Baltimore

Printed in the United States of America

I dedicate this story to my mother Edith O'Connor, who loved a good story and told me many a tall tale when I was growing up.

And my husband Robert, who has always encouraged me to expand my mind and write from my heart, never forgetting the passion.

Are women less secure because of poor feedback?

Is it because mothers and society as a whole revere men, expecting only the best from them and disregard the talents and abilities of women?

Excerpt from Patricia O'Connor's book
HOW TO SURVIVE YOUR MOTHER'S LOVE

ACKNOWLEDGMENTS

My sincere thanks to John Atkinson, a young Englishman, for his sterling editing contributions to this story, he is one of the best editors a writer could have.

He encouraged me to go the extra yard in writing a story I could be really proud of.

CHAPTER 1

July 1979
Inish Mann, Aran Isles:

The young woman drifted in and out of consciousness, her long auburn hair soaked with blood and mist from the sea. She forced her eyes open and tried to sit up. She could hear the muffled sounds of the sea crashing against the rocks below and closer still the sounds of a violent struggle. Her vision was hazy and her head throbbed with pain. She must have passed out after she tried to stop the fight and was pushed back against the rocks. She touched the side of her face. It was wet with blood and there was some on her lips. When she licked them the taste made her feel nauseous.

The sound of the brawl moved even closer; her father Edward Ryan and Tim O'Shea were still locked in battle. It was obvious that Tim was tiring fast and her father, a head taller than his opponent, was the stronger of the two men.

She screamed at them to stop but the waves deadened the sound of her voice and the battle raged on. Why had her father attacked Tim? Why hadn't he listened when she tried to explain that the young man was just a friend? It hadn't helped that he had caught Tim trying to kiss her.

Jacqueline couldn't understand why Tim had suddenly decided to force his attentions on her. She was his best friend's girl and as far as she was concerned they were nothing more than social friends.

She watched, powerless as her father continued to beat the young man senseless. Tim staggered back over a rock and lost his balance. His head hit the ground and the rocks beneath him turned crimson with blood. Then he stopped moving.

A look of horror flickered across her father's face and he hesitated, breathing heavily. He glanced around, not noticing his daughter's eyes on him. Then, as she watched, he moved cagily towards the young man, leaned over him, checked his pulse and then picked him up, half dragging, half carrying him towards the edge of the cliff. He then heaved the body over the side, gravity plunging it into the raging seas below.

Jacqueline struggled against the power of the wind that tried to push her back, moving closer to where her father stood. She screamed at him.

"You've killed him. You're a murderer."

He turned, shocked. He had forgotten she was there watching him. Then he moved threateningly towards her and she became afraid. She backed away, moving ever closer to the edge of the cliff; she was screaming for help, crying out for someone, anyone, who might hear her.

The wind and the crash of the waves muffled her cries. The last thing she remembered was his huge hand pressed firmly over her mouth.

CHAPTER 2

January 2004

London Fashion Week was in full swing. It was one of the city's biggest attractions and key fashion leaders from around the world were in attendance, promoting their new designs. The glamorous event brought together celebrities and would-be celebrities from many countries.

Sixties rockers like Mick Jagger, Paul McCartney, Roger Daltry and others, now multi-millionaire come-back kids, are given carte blanche at such events and their attendance is always in demand.

A number of lesser-known young musicians also attended these occasions. Most of them had beautiful young women hanging on their arms; the women, more often than not, ex-models or would-be actresses. You could spot them by the nervous way they checked out the rest of the female competition and made sure their hard-earned boyfriends didn't stray too far from their sides.

The paparazzi watched the cat-and-mouse games as they played out. They stalked their prey for problems, heartlessly hunting for a scrap of news or different angle to a story. If they could only latch onto a love affair or break-up before someone else, they could earn a packet and perhaps achieve their fifteen minutes of fame. Individuals who attended these shows were of great interest to the public at large. The right celebrity photograph could be worth a small fortune to a photographer. Hence, the hungry snappers had to be on the ball, clued up on the new wave of television and movie stars—and ready to pounce when they surfaced.

So much of the public lived their lives vicariously through celebrities. They wanted to know everything about them; what they wore, how they looked, if they had gained or lost weight and what was going on in their love-lives.

This was the last in a series of fifty catwalk programmes on the London Fashion Week schedule. The mood in the room was filled with anticipation as the live band began a sensual beat and the lights in the hall slowly dimmed.

One large pink spotlight followed a spectacular looking young red-haired model as she moved gracefully along the runway. Annie O'Hanlon enjoyed the hum of excitement and the sound of the 'Oohs' and 'Aahs' as she let the high-priced sable coat she was wearing slip from her slim shoulders and trail behind along the runway. Beneath the coat she wore a long peach satin gown with a halter-top and low back. It clung to her stunning young body like a second skin.

She dragged the fur as though it were a rag until she reached the end of the runway, then, moving centre stage, she casually tossed the coat away and turned towards the audience with a mischievous smile and took an exaggerated bow. The crowd went wild and she left the runway to applause and catcalls.

She smiled as she made her way towards her dressing room. It was fun using the acting techniques she had learned at RADA. As a teenager she dreamt of becoming an actress and attended acting courses in London.

She changed direction when she was offered a lucrative modelling contract but had still continued her acting classes. Her drama background hadn't been wasted. Training was essential and gave you an edge when you were competing with other models. It was a very competitive business.

She was now twenty-five and one of the highest paid models in the business. And she also owned a small premiere cosmetic company. It was her pension for the future.

Annie began modelling at seventeen. It was her spectacular red hair, height, curvy body and a lot of hard work (mainly the hard work) that made her a supermodel. Most of the girls were very thin, some merely skin and bone.

Annie was proud of her curvy body. Few men bothered with skinny models that looked like boys. She got a lot of positive attention from both straight and gay men, and the women in the audience related to her, too. It had taken years of sacrifice and hard work to make it to the top.

As she left the runway she gave her head a really good scratch. It felt *so* good. Christine her hair stylist was watching and ran to her side.

"Annie, stop it...don't...you'll ruin it...stop scratching your head this minute!"

The stylist had spent what seemed like hours working on the hairstyle. It had been backcombed endlessly and French braided, not an easy job with such thick auburn hair; and then she had strategically placed two diamond clips, worth a small fortune, in the front.

Christine knew that, because of those diamonds, Annie would be the most photographed and talked-about model in the next morning's papers. She would be seen on TV—and probably on the front pages of a number of fashion journals—wearing Christine's hairstyle. At the moment the model was the flavour of the month and the photographers couldn't seem to get enough of the smarmy bitch.

She gave Annie another warning look as the model touched her hair, trying desperately to control the urge to scratch it.

Fashion could be a right, royal pain in the arse. That was one of the reasons Annie had decided to get out of it this year and move full-time into the cosmetics business.

The age restriction for models was another good reason to get out now. At twenty-five she was already considered one of the more mature models in the business. Most of the girls she worked with were in their teens, some as young as fourteen. Periodically, she worked with women who were still modelling well into their mid-thirties. They had once been super-models and most of them had already gone under the knife to compete with the latest crop of beautiful young girls half their age.

Annie felt sorry for them and thought they looked a little desperate. The work really took a lot out of a person. The general public only saw the finished product. They had no idea what went into a show or a photo shoot.

A model could spend days and sometimes weeks before a show, being draped and pinned—and then re-draped—into the latest fashions. Designers had a habit of changing their minds about their creations and a model was expected to look beautiful and interested and stand still for hours while they worked and reworked the garment on her. And she was expected to make suggestions and answer questions about the feel of the garment and the fit.

Annie couldn't recall the number of hours she had spent being fitted or the amount of times she was stuck with pins because of some careless designer's assistant; there was also the small matter of the stiff and achy joints she suffered during those fittings.

Then there was the make-up you had to endure. It got freakier every year. Some stylists were worse than others, not giving a damn how a model felt or looked. To them you were nothing more than a human canvas.

She could never understand why they insisted on hiring the most beautiful girl they could find…and then spend hours turning the poor woman into some hideous, lifeless-looking creature.

The most unpleasant make-up artists were the ones who thought they could make a name for themselves by creating some weird new look. In her years as a model Annie had suffered through it all. She couldn't remember how many colours her face had been painted. The dead white Kabuki make-up was the worst. It had a thick oil base and made her skin break out and her eyes swell up. The stylists didn't care about the after-effects of their creations, as long as it worked for their shows. It took weeks of trips to the dermatologist and a lot of downtime before her skin and eyes were back to normal.

It also took a huge amount of time and energy to prepare for shows and photo shoots. Yes, modelling was definitely best suited to the very young.

She had decided she would get out when she turned twenty-five and the cosmetics industry was her answer. She had already made enough money to last a lifetime. Money was not the issue. Thank goodness this was her last year in the business. She was really sick of modelling and some of the strange people it attracted.

Her large, hazel eyes clouded over as she recalled the New York designer who wanted her to model his collection stark naked. Generally, she had no problem with nudity, so long as the garments covered one's 'assets'. When you worked a big runway show with numerous outfits to change into, there wasn't enough time to change your underwear; and, sure, sometimes her breasts did show through a gauzy top. But this was different.

The first half of his collection was unlike anything Annie had ever worn and, when she tried the clothes on, she was shocked. The garments were made of the sheerest white gauze fabric she had ever seen. You could literally see everything through them; yes, *everything*.

She guessed he was trying to make a statement, but what on earth could it be? And she had also learned from one of the stylists that a number of the Kennedy family, the cream of American society, were to be seated in the front row, along with six Irish nuns they had brought with them. Annie wondered if the designer had finally lost his marbles.

He was furious with her when she said she had no intention of modelling his collection unless she was allowed to wear a neutral body stocking under them. She was his main model and he didn't have time to get a substitute, so he didn't have a choice and went along with her demands.

Annie didn't care what he thought of her, she had no intention of ever working for the disgusting little man again.

They were all staying at the same hotel and her room was right next to his. There was a lot of noise coming from his room later that night and the next day one of the hotel staff told her that the designer shared his suite with a young gay man and a pre-teen French girl. Annie guessed he was bi-sexual. She knew that he was married to a very pretty American film star and they had children together. She felt sorry for his wife and wondered if she knew exactly the kind of man she'd married.

It was odd; the very attributes that had made her a supermodel had caused her nothing but pain as a child. She would never forget the unkind taunts and remarks of the kids in her neighbourhood in Dublin. They had ruined her childhood and made her life a living hell.

Her height had caused Annie the most pain. By the time she was twelve she was five foot eleven and the Irish kids, generally short, delighted in calling her a host of offensive names; 'Frankenstein's daughter' and 'Freak' among them. She had even suffered name-calling from her younger brother and sister who were both short. Why was she so tall when everyone else in her family was short? It was something she couldn't understand.

When she was thirteen she was so concerned about her height that she decided to save up for an operation she had read about in a magazine. It was a new procedure and the doctor who had pioneered it claimed he could shorten a person's legs by between two to four inches. She wrote to the company and, when the promotion material arrived in the post, learned they would have to cut off both legs, shorten them and then reattach them. She quickly changed her mind. She shivered now at the very thought of it.

As she moved down the runway for the second time, wearing a pink tweed Chanel dress and jacket and two-tone shoes, she pondered.

Grown-ups had no idea how much pain children suffered through name-calling. She wondered where the children were now who had been so unkind to her. What had become of them? She smiled, as she moved gracefully along the catwalk, humming: "If they could see me now…"

A photographer caught her on camera and gave her a wink.

CHAPTER 3

The smartly-dressed young woman leaving the elegant Victorian building on O'Connell Street in Dublin was annoyed to see two scruffy-looking men standing directly in front of the door, partially blocking her exit.

She mouthed: "Excuse me," pushed past the men and moved quickly away as if she might catch something from them. One of the two men was a young journalist. He looked edgy as his fingers tightened round a fistful of banknotes.

He was roughly dressed in an old beige tweed jacket and grey woollen trousers that had seen better days. He was busy questioning an even scruffier-looking older man. The man was a snitch with news to sell. The reporter knew that, given half a chance, the man would sell his own mother to the highest bidder. But then, the material he'd purchased from Graves in the past had always panned out.

This time it was so important that what he was to learn from the man was correct. Dermot's goal was to become a serious journalist and his future could hang on this information. If what Graves had told him was true, he had the story of a lifetime—and his editor would stop treating him like a cub reporter. At last he'd be able to name his own terms at the newspaper. But if it was just a pack of lies…a shudder went through him.

"Are you sure?" he asked anxiously for the fifth time.

The older man looked angry. Why didn't the fat bastard believe him? If a certain person spotted him talking to the reporter he'd be dead meat; but he needed the money. He took a shot of whisky to steady his nerves. His hands had already begun to shake.

He shivered in the cold morning air and tugged the soiled collar of his raincoat higher up around his face. He couldn't afford to be seen talking to a reporter. He studied the lunchtime crowd nervously. He should never have agreed to meet him here; it was madness to take such a chance.

It was Moore who had insisted they meet outside the building. Why had he agreed? If he weren't careful they'd find his body floating in the River Liffey in the morning.

"For God's sake man," he begged, his voice was raw with emotion. "How many times do I have to tell you? I saw the woman at Rosemont Hospital! It was her alright."

Dermot hesitated, momentarily loosening his grip on the money as the man pressed home his information. "I swear to you, I'm telling you the truth."

Then the old man took a chance, made a grab for the money and, in a second, was gone, swallowed up by the lunchtime crowds.

The journalist studied the passers-by and straightened his jacket. He tried to button it, forgetting that the jacket was too tight. He'd gained about sixty pounds and none of his clothes fitted him properly. He'd have to go on another bloody diet!

He hesitated for a couple of seconds, then, with a shrug, pushed open the elaborate double-doors of 'RYAN AND RYAN, ATTORNEYS AT LAW'.

A woman, with the air of a matron, was seated behind the reception desk. She was busy reading a newspaper. She looked up as he entered. But he didn't fit the type of person she was used to dealing with, so she resumed her reading, periodically glancing up with a look of dislike as the man waited.

Her face said it all.

She clearly had no intention of dealing with him. The nerve of the man, coming into a business establishment dressed in an old frayed jacket.

If she had looked hard enough she could have seen parts of his hairy chest peeking out between the buttons of his untidy plaid shirt. Young people today...honestly.

Dermot gave her his warmest smile.

"Good morning..."

She ignored him and continued reading her paper.

"Bloody old hag," he thought, feeling slighted. Then he shrugged his shoulders and raised his voice.

"I'm Dermot Moore from the Irish Star. I'm here to see Edward Ryan..."

A security guard next to the reception desk studied him suspiciously. The man had the appearance of a retired police officer and he made Dermot nervous.

"I *do* have an appointment..."

He hated the way his voice sounded trying to convince the ignorant sods that he should be there.

The woman was still ignoring him and it was the security guard who finally picked up the telephone and slowly, but deliberately, dialled a number.

"There's a man down here, sir...says he's from *The Star*...says he has an appointment. His name is Moore."

The response he received appeared to take him by complete surprise and he turned to face the reporter.

"Yes sir, right away, sir. I'll send him right up."

He gestured towards the lift.

"Top floor..."

Once inside the lift, Dermot practised again what he was going to say, how he might open the conversation. But the lift came to a stop almost immediately and the doors opened silently into a large reception area that screamed understated elegance and *money*.

Dermot's size 13 feet sank quietly into the plush carpet. He couldn't help being impressed by the rich furnishings and the large rosewood antique reception desk in front of him. The room had obviously been furnished to impress clients.

A conventionally dressed young woman greeted him with a smile that didn't quite reach her eyes. Her voice (like the clothes she wore) was cool and efficient, and it was obvious she didn't intend wasting a minute more on him than she had to.

"Mr. Ryan is expecting you. Please follow me."

He followed her, as she strode quickly down the hallway, and helped her push open one of the heavy ornate double doors into the man's office. She motioned him to go ahead of her and followed him into the inner sanctum of one of Ireland's most powerful barristers.

Edward Ryan had made a fortune, as well as a name for himself, representing powerful politicians and white-collar criminals. Dermot had been very thorough with his research and had learned that Ryan could be a formidable opponent in court. The man had won endless legal battles for his wealthy clients.

But when Dermot had contacted some of Ryan's clients, they appeared nervous and uncomfortable talking about the barrister and refused to be interviewed. Dermot figured that a lot of powerful people owed Ryan favours.

The receptionist cleared her throat.

"Err…Mr Ryan…"

She waited for a response but he ignored her and continued reading his newspaper.

"Dermot Moore here to see you, sir…"

She looked uncomfortable as she waited for a response from her boss but he continued to ignore them both.

It gave Dermot time to study the man. He saw that everything about Ryan was designed to impress; from the top of his stylish silver hair to the monogrammed deep blue shirt and the expensive dark blue pinstriped Saville Row jacket that hung on the back of his chair. Dermot noted the expensive Rolex watch on his wrist and a heavy gold university ring on one of the stubby, carefully manicured fingers of his left hand. The man reeked of success and money.

The secretary decided she had waited long enough and left the room, closing the door quietly behind her.

Dermot fidgeted; his throat felt dry and he tried to clear it as he moved nervously towards Ryan's desk. He wished he felt more in control and confident—and not so bloody tense.

Edward Ryan looked up and pointed to a plush rose-coloured chair the other side of his desk.

"For God's sake man, sit down and stop fidgeting."

Relieved, Dermot let his bulk sink heavily into the luxurious armchair. Ryan smiled at him, showing off a set of perfect white teeth.

"I gather you're here to do an interview on me."

Ryan's smile lit up his handsome, suntanned face and the young journalist got his first glimpse of the charisma of the man he was dealing with. The large hazel eyes studied the journalist enquiringly.

"If you need background information, my secretary Deirdre can get it for you."

Dermot decided to lower his voice, to hide a nervous quiver.

"You've, err, got it wrong, sir. I'm not here to interview you. I'm, err…here to get some questions answered."

Ryan looked surprised and he cursed himself for being a fool. What had he let himself in for with this rookie reporter? But his voice sounded cool and measured.

"And what are these questions you want answered?"

Dermot replied quickly so he wouldn't sound so nervous.

"I…would like some information regarding the whereabouts of your daughter Jacqueline. I've been told you placed her in a mental institution—after she got pregnant at sixteen. I want to know why, and also if there is any truth in…"

Before Dermot could complete his sentence, Ryan had leapt from his chair, darted around his desk and grabbed the journalist by the throat. His hands were like steel. With a look of pure hatred his hands tightened around the young man's throat and he hissed: "You bastard. I'll bloody kill you!"

Dermot made a gagging sound as he struggled frantically to pull the man's hands away. He couldn't get his breath and the room had begun to spin around him. Too late, he realized that he had enraged Ryan to the point of murder.

Then, just as unexpectedly as the attack had begun, the older man relaxed his grip and, like a rag doll, the reporter slid to the floor. A second later Ryan was back in his seat and appeared to have regained his composure. He then asked another question as if nothing had happened.

"What's this all about then?"

Dermot struggled desperately to regain control of his senses. He was still shaking as he got to his knees and somehow managed to flop back into the chair. He paused, straightened his clothes and rubbed his sore throat.

"I have information from a reliable source…" he said delicately, not wanting to set the man off again. He watched the older man carefully now. Ryan's eyes belied the tone of his voice; they were filled with hate.

Dermot continued to speak softly.

"I have evidence that, twenty-five years ago, you had your daughter committed to a mental hospital after she became pregnant."

Edward Ryan was fuming. *What did this rookie really know about 'Jacqueline'? He should have controlled his temper. Now the reporter would guess that he had something to hide, he would know that something was going on. Who had, Moran, spoken to? He decided to bluff it out.*

"You and your so-called evidence, it's nothing but a load of old bullshit! My guess is you got your information from some small-time crook. My daughter Jacqueline is dead. She drowned in a boating accident off Inish Mann."

Then he rose from his desk and, with a look that could kill and a voice full of spite, he added: "You won't get away with this. I plan on contacting your editor regarding these libellous comments."

He pressed a concealed button under his desk and, within seconds, two tough-looking men appeared in the doorway. Ryan gestured to Dermot.

"I want you to show this...err...gentleman out, before I throw him out."

CHAPTER 4

Fashion Week was almost over and a number of young men and women from various Art & Design schools still hung around, dreaming of the day it might be their turn. A group of what-used-to-be-called 'Stage-Door Johnnies' were also present. They filled the hallways, waiting impatiently for the models and celebrities to leave.

The backstage dressing room was still crowded with models in various stages of undress. Annie and her roommate Terri were busy removing their make-up in front of the mirror.

Annie glanced at her friend in the mirror.

"I was really proud of you tonight, Terri. It's hard to believe you're the same girl I met two years ago at the hospital."

Annie was part of a women's help group working with battered women and it was exactly two years since she'd received a frantic call from Mrs Porter at the women's refuge regarding Terri. Mrs Porter ran the home.

A young woman had just been rushed into Emergency and needed their help. When Annie arrived, Mrs Porter answered the door. She was a kind, rotund woman, in her late fifties, who had not been blessed with children of her own. As a result, she felt particularly maternal towards the young women in her care. It broke her heart when one of them didn't make it, because of drugs or a brutal beating at the hands of some man.

Her face looked sad and her eyes filled with tears as she took Annie's arm.

"Thank God you're here. I'm afraid the poor girl may not last the night. She's been beaten to within an inch of her life. That husband of hers must be an out-and-out sadist to hurt such a lovely young woman…"

Sadly Annie had seen it all before. She followed Mrs Porter into a small side room where the young woman lay on a narrow hospital bed. Her face was a mass of bruises; both eyes were swollen shut and had started to turn blue, and her blonde hair was caked with blood. Teresa Dunne's breathing was also very laboured.

Mrs Porter pulled back the sheet to expose the naked body covered in bruises and welts. "He's broken several of her ribs," she said, covering the young woman and gently stroking her head.

Annie turned to her, seething with anger, and fumed: "Has he been here yet? Has he tried to see her?"

Mrs Porter shook her head.

"He wouldn't dare show his face. If he did, I'd have the police on him so fast it would make his head spin."

Terri's husband James had been violently jealous of his beautiful young wife and had lost his temper during what started as a trivial argument. It wasn't the first time he had beaten her, but this time he nearly killed her.

Annie stayed with Terri most of that night and Terri said she had had enough. She now feared for her life and wanted out of her marriage. She was afraid her husband would eventually kill her if she returned to him. When she was eventually released from the hospital, Annie found her a safe place to live and set about helping her regain her self-confidence.

It was three months before the bruises healed completely and her face and body looked normal again, and during that time the two women became firm friends. By now they shared a three-bedroom apartment in London's Mayfair district.

Annie had also helped Terri find work as a model. It hadn't been difficult. She was tall, slim, and blonde, and bore an uncanny resemblance to the young Grace Kelly. It was really just a matter of giving her some modelling tips and introducing her to the right people.

Their friendship had changed both of their lives for the better; Terri adored Annie, who was like an older sister to her.

"I don't know what I would have done without you," Terri said, recollecting. "You helped me regain my life."

She looked thoughtful. "I was such a fool. James used me as his private punching bag and I let him. I thought he would change because he said he loved me and was always promising he wouldn't do it again."

Annie nodded.

Terri looked sad.

"I don't know what was wrong with me, I must have been sick in the head or something…To think I actually married the bastard. I'm so glad you came to the hospital and talked me into contacting the police," she said, sounding anxious.

"I still have nightmares about what he might do when he gets out of prison. He swore he'd kill us both!"

Men like James had threatened Annie in the past, when she helped their wives or girlfriends. She wasn't the least bit afraid of him or worried he might hurt her. Her past experience had taught her that men who attacked women were all cowards at heart.

She appeared wistful.

"He's all talk. Any man who beats up a woman is nothing but a spineless coward. I'm not scared of him."

Terri decided to change the subject. She hated thinking about James and what might have been if he had been a different sort of man.

"I pick up the contract for my TV commercial tomorrow. If you've got time, will you take a look at it for me?"

Annie nodded, smiling. They were still in the changing room, which was now almost empty. Terri glanced affectionately at her friend as she slipped a short black Chanel gown over her head.

Annie could just as easily have been a solicitor. A few years earlier she'd invested in a course on contract law, having been cheated too many times by unscrupulous individuals.

Surprisingly she had taken to the course like a duck to water and really enjoyed it. Her instructor was so impressed he tried to talk her into becoming a solicitor. The course gave her a new level of confidence and no one messed with her anymore.

She smiled at her friend.

"Of course I'll check out your contract. Now get ready, Mrs Porter is throwing a birthday party in your honour, missy."

Terri stuck out her tongue and they laughed.

"I know how much you hate birthdays but remember, you're not getting older, you're getting better."

Terri giggled. "We won't stay long," Annie said. "I want us to look really fantastic tomorrow for the photo shoot. After all, we'll be promoting my very own make-up line."

Mrs Porter lived in Chiswick with her banker, husband, John.

There was a great deal of history in the Chiswick area. The original Roman Road from London passed through there and, some seventeen centuries after it was built, the nephew of King Charles I, Prince Rupert, retreated along it after eight hundred of his Cavaliers were massacred by Cromwell's Roundheads.

At the time, living in a big city (London in particular), was a distinctly hazardous situation. Health was of primary consideration in the selection of Chiswick for the new estate. Situated upon a gravel-bed close to the Thames, its drainage was excellent, and it was largely unaffected by the dense fogs that descended over London and contributed to the lung and chest diseases that were prevalent at that time.

Mrs Porter owned a large Victorian house. The area still retained its original identity thanks to being placed in the historical registry. This was once a popular area for artists and writers. The room where the party was held was very spacious and about fifty people were already there, milling from room to room in the old Victorian house.

By the time Annie and Terri got to the birthday party it was in full swing. A number of women they modelled with were there, along with some make-up artists and hairstylists they worked with regularly. The moment they entered the room a trio began playing "Happy Birthday to you," as Terry blushed with embarrassment.

A little while later Annie and Mrs Porter were busy chatting when Mrs Porter said:

"I think Terri has a crush on someone, she's been checking the room a lot."

Annie looked over to where Terri stood. She had a glass of Champagne in her hand and Annie realized Mrs Porter was right, *She was checking the room for someone; but who was she looking for, who could the man be?*

Terri glanced around the room, scanning the crowd for the one man she hoped might attend her party. Then the bell rang and minutes later he appeared. When she saw him she felt her face flush and tried desperately to hide the excitement she felt at his arrival. Annie was watching her friend's reaction to Christian. He was the director of Annie's cosmetic company. And she felt relieved Terri was interested in men again; and she had a thing for Christian. She could understand her friend's interest; Christian was a handsome man. He was exceptionally tall—at least six four—but he moved gracefully. His hair was dark blonde and there was usually a twinkle in his blue eyes, as if he was constantly thinking of something humorous to say.

He turned heads as he made his way through the crowd towards Terri. She was chatting with Mrs Porter and Annie when the handsome young man finally reached her side. He handed her a large bouquet of red roses and then as Frenchmen do, he kissed her on both cheeks. It was a friendly kiss, nothing more; but Annie noticed that her friend's face turned bright red at his touch. Then the lights went out as the enormous birthday cake covered with sparklers headed in their direction. Annie noticed that Christian stayed by Terri's side as she blew out her candles. And when the dance music began, they were in each other's arms.

CHAPTER 5

Michael O'Brien, the editor of *The Star* newspaper, was feeling particularly angry at the travesty he was obliged to carry out with Dermot Moore, his rookie reporter.

"What in God's name were you thinking of, Dermot?"

He studied the untidy looking young man in front of him. It was a shame he had to let him go, as Dermot was actually quite a talented writer. O'Brien tried to summon up some anger.

"Accusing a man like Edward Ryan before clearing it with me?"

Dermot looked sheepish.

"I wanted to expose what he did to his daughter. The public deserves to know the truth."

Michael stopped Dermot in mid-sentence.

"And are you absolutely sure you know the truth? Some old drunk sells you a story and you believe him? Don't you know how powerful Edward Ryan is?"

Dermot shrugged his shoulders.

"So…are you saying that the laws that apply to us don't apply to him because he's rich and powerful?"

He continued angrily: "What about his daughter's rights? She's been locked away for twenty-five years."

Michael handed Dermot an old edition of *The Star's* obituary column and pointed to the paper.

"Did you bother to read this before you went to see Ryan? It clearly states that his daughter Jacqueline lost her life in a boating accident in 1973. It was off the Aran Isles and she was with a young man at the time."

Dermot glanced at the newspaper. He was unimpressed.

"That doesn't mean anything...It also says that they only recovered the man's body, the girl's body was never found. I'm telling you, Michael, I believe Graves. He swore he saw her at Rosemont Hospital. I've bought stuff from him in the past and it's always panned out. He's a good snitch."

Michael was frustrated at the turn the conversation had taken. In his heart he knew the young reporter was right to follow-up on the story, he would have done the same twenty years ago. Twenty years ago he was a struggling young reporter, not unlike Dermot, anxious to make a name for himself. He used to imagine receiving the Pulitzer Prize for his writing. But things were different now; he was married and had five children to support, so he couldn't afford such foolishness.

Just before the meeting with Dermot, he had received a telephone call from Edward Ryan, who insisted he fire the reporter. Michael didn't like being told what to do or whom he should fire. He was the editor, for God's sake, not Ryan. But if he supported the young journalist over Ryan, he was sure to lose everything himself. He couldn't afford to go back to reporting. And he couldn't go up against a man like Ryan, he was way too powerful.

The man owned a lot of people; he was even on the board of *The Star*. If Michael didn't roll over and do as he was told he could find himself out the door, along with Moore. And then what would his family do?

He felt sad as he studied the young journalist. He just couldn't take a chance; he would have to fire him.

"I still say you should have checked it out with me first, Dermot. I'm sorry, but I'm going to have to let you go. You're...err...a loose cannon. The paper can't afford you or your potential legal bills."

CHAPTER 6

Early the next morning, Annie and Terri were at The Langham hotel for the photo shoot. They were staying there for two nights. Annie had picked that particular hotel because of its period look. It was one of London's first grand hotels and had a wonderful feel about it. It had been restored to its original Edwardian splendour and she loved its understated elegance. The hotel conveyed exactly the feeling of luxury and quality that she wanted to use to promote her products.

She was passionate about her skin-care line and wanted people who bought her products to feel pampered and get the right results when they used them. She had spent a lot of time and money making sure the products did exactly what they promised. From the time she was in her teens, she had experimented with lotions and makeup and knew what worked and what didn't.

Two years earlier, with a concept of what she wanted her skin-care and make-up line to achieve and a good deal of money to spend, she had hired a brilliant young French chemist who worked endlessly with her until he came up with the correct formulas.

As a result, her products really did do what they claimed. And, when her customers saw their skin had clearly improved, success quickly followed. The line was now on sale at Harrods in London and at top department stores throughout Europe.

The original containers had begun to look a little dated, so Annie had hired a clever young designer to come up with a fresh and attractive new design. The packaging now came in pale rose and gold, giving it an elegant yet antique look.

Joanne, her make-up artist, decided that the models should look strong yet feminine and wear colours that complemented the packaging. Three models were being used for the photo shoot, Terri, Annie and Maura, a girl of seventeen who was hired to represent the teen market.

They arrived at the make-up room in their bathrobes with clean, shiny faces. Joanne and her assistant Stephanie were already waiting for them and got to work right away. Two hours later they were ready.

The first part of the day was a bit of a disaster. They were scheduled to shoot some of the scenes in the hotel entrance but the rain bucketed down and it had to be cancelled. They decided to move the shoot inside, but that didn't work as the hotel staff had problems keeping curious onlookers away.

To eliminate the problems, their director, Christian, decided to film the bath products first, so all of the equipment, products, and costumes were moved into one of the penthouse suites. He would photograph Terri first, in an old-fashioned bathtub with ornate claw feet.

Stephanie helped her out of her fluffy white robe and she slid into the foamy warm water, the foamy bubbles hiding the more intimate parts of her body. Christian lit her with a soft rose-toned light that made her skin look luminous.

The stylist had pinned up Terri's long blonde hair with deep plum-coloured ribbons and a large pink rose. Both Christian and Annie were delighted with the results. Then it was Annie's turn.

The stylist felt she should be photographed next to the fireplace in the bedroom. She wore a full-length plum-coloured satin gown that hugged her body in all the right places and looked spectacular against her porcelain skin and red hair. Joanne had slicked Annie's hair away from her face and into a tight knot at the back, emphasizing her remarkable hazel eyes and delicate bone structure.

The effect was exactly what they'd been looking for. The gown and her full rose-tinted mouth had turned her into one of the heroines from a period romance. Several of the crew commented that Annie reminded them of Vivian Leigh in 'Gone with the Wind'. Christian shot her in the stunning bedroom, standing next to an elegant Edwardian fireplace. The effect was both romantic and sensual at the same time.

The time flew by and, at one o'clock; Christian called for a lunch break, telling them all to be back by 2.30pm. Terri told Annie she was going shopping for something special to wear that night; Christian had asked her out to dinner.

Annie was delighted. She knew the man had a crush on Terri, and realised that her friend was interested in Christian too. He'd be good for her; he was a kind man who genuinely liked women. She had watched him at work with her staff and, although some of them would have tested the patience of Job with their inane questions, Christian never lost his patience or temper. She knew Terri would be safe with him.

Although Annie was exhausted, she still felt hyper and couldn't rest from the morning's activities. She went up to her room, telephoned room service and ordered a tuna sandwich and coffee. Then she sat and studied the following afternoon's shooting schedule until her food arrived. The waiter set the tray on the table next to the window. He studied the beautiful young model as he arranged her food. "Is there anything else you would like Miss?" he asked, running his eyes over the young woman's spectacular body, fantasizing, *like a date or maybe a quickie right here on your bed?*

" No, nothing else," She replied, handing him a five-pound tip, as she closed the door firmly behind him.

She was starving and devoured her sandwich in-between sipping the scalding coffee. Then she ran a bath, hoping it would help her relax. She added a dash of her new bath oil to the water.

She was about to step into the inviting foamy waters when the telephone rang. It was her mother calling from Ireland and it sounded as if she'd been crying. Before Annie could ask what was wrong she blurted out: "Annie darling, Daddy's had a heart attack. I need you, can you come home right away?"

Annie was too shocked to answer; it took a moment for her to grasp what her mother had just said. The voice continued anxiously.

"Are you there, dear, did you hear me?"

And, as if in a dream, she replied: "Yes, I heard you. Is he going to be alright?"

A stifled sob was the only answer she got in return and Annie panicked.

"Mammy, please tell me he's OK, that he's still alive…"

As she asked the question she prayed that the answer would be *yes*, but between sobs her mother cried out a response to the contrary.

"No…no…I thought you understood…HE'S GONE…he's dead."

She murmured quietly as if she was trying to understand it herself.

"He wasn't even sick; I never knew he had a heart problem."

When Annie was finally able to think clearly, she realized that the photo shoot would have to go on without her. She would have to leave for Ireland that evening and Terri and Maura would have to finish the photo shoot without her. Her eyes were red and swollen from crying. She was in no condition to face a camera.

Later that day Terri drove her to Heathrow Airport to get a flight to Dublin. As they walked towards the departure lounge, they linked arms.

"I'm so glad you were able to bring me to the airport," Annie said.

Then she turned towards Terry. "Let's have a cup of tea before I leave; we have time, the flight doesn't leave for another forty minutes and my bags are already on board. I have something I want to ask you."

As they walked toward the coffee shop, Terri wondered what Annie wanted? They grabbed a cup of tea and sat at a table that someone else had just left. It was covered in used napkins and empty coffee cups. Without thinking, Annie cleared it off and dumped the mess in the bin. Then she sat and sipped her tea as she studied her friend.

"What would you think about handling my cosmetics company while I'm in Ireland?"

Terri was thrilled with the idea and told her friend she would love to oversee the business. She had never admitted it to Annie, but she, too, wasn't crazy about the modelling side of the business. She had gone along with it because of the money she could make. Like Annie, she had always loved working with cosmetics.

Annie knew she would feel a lot better leaving for Ireland knowing that Terri would be keeping an eye on things. She had a terrific group of people working for her; they were all outgoing people-oriented individuals. She had been very lucky and managed to hire patient and caring men and women who liked bringing out the best in customers.

Her company in Britain manufactured and tested her products, and she had a number of well-trained sales girls who represented her cosmetic line, in various top stores in London and Europe. Terri would fit right in; as she studied her friend she knew that Terri would be an asset to any company.

"I feel better knowing you'll be running things while I'm away," she said.

"And I know that Christian will be there to give you a hand."

But a tear came to her eye as she remembered the reason she was leaving. Terri handed her a tissue.

"Are you sure you'll be OK?"

Annie nodded.

"Yes, but I still can't believe that Daddy's gone. He was only fifty-three and had always seemed so healthy. He played tennis three times a week."

Terri stroked her hand sympathetically.

"He looked so well when I saw him last, I thought I'd have him around for at least another 20 years."

They finished their tea and left the coffee shop, heading for the *Passengers Only* area. After they hugged goodbye, Terri took a tissue and wiped a bit of mascara off her friend's cheek.

"Try to remember the good times you had together and how much he loved you," she whispered as she gave Annie a final hug.

On the short flight to Ireland, Annie did what Terri suggested, recalling some of the good times she had spent with her father. John O'Hanlon was a good man and a wonderful father. The strange thing was that she had always felt much closer to him than she did to her mother. She didn't know why, but she and her mother never really got on. Whenever they were together she got the feeling that, no matter how hard she tried, she would always be a disappointment. Her brother and sister received lots of hugs and kisses from their mother when they were growing up, but Annie felt she had always received the short end of the stick as far as maternal love was concerned.

She wasn't jealous of the affection her mother showered on her longhaired younger brother, who was crazy about music and wanted to become a rock star, or her slightly chubby younger teenage sister. She had never begrudged them the love her mother lavished on them. She just wished there had been more left over for her.

But her father was always there to make up for her mother's shortcomings. Annie remembered some of the early Sunday mornings they spent together when she was a child, picking blackberries in the foothills of the Wicklow Mountains. Her father insisted they be out of the house by six; he told her that blackberries were best with the dew still on them. By the time they finished nibbling and filling their baskets to the top with the delicious fruit, the brambles had often scratched them to bits. They would head home weary and her mother would set about making them her delicious blackberry and apple pies.

Annie didn't know why, but her father always appeared more relaxed when they were alone. He was great fun and would let his hair down and act the goat with her. She remembered the time they had rented roller skates in the Phoenix Park. They hadn't made allowances for the hills and almost ended up in the duck pond!

She smiled, recalling the way he watched over her and how protective he became when she started dating boys.

Then there was the time he mentioned the other woman in his life. They had just finished picking blackberries and were enjoying afternoon tea in the little café in Bray, when he said he had been there before; that he had brought 'another young woman' to that very same café.

Annie was surprised at his confession. He told her the woman was another beautiful redhead—but the place looked different then.

"Things do look different you know, when you're in love," he whispered wistfully.

Figuring that this 'grand affair' was before he met her mother, she let the subject drop. But she couldn't help remembering the look on his face when he reminisced about that woman.

Now that he was gone, everything would be so different at home; she would sorely miss their long chats on the telephone each Friday. She wouldn't be able to call him like she used to, give him all the latest news and listen to his funny Irish jokes. Nothing would ever be the same again.

CHAPTER 7

The voice of the Aer Lingus flight attendant came over the plane's intercom and broke the spell. They would be landing in five minutes. As they finally came to a halt and the cabin door was opened, Annie left the plane as quickly as she could and headed for the baggage area. She got a baggage cart and followed the dozens of people heading towards their carousel.

It seemed an eternity before the conveyor belt began to move. It always seemed so slow when you were in a hurry. Annie spotted her two pieces of luggage right away, pulled them free and loaded them onto her trolley. She was soon through the door and pushing through the crowds waiting for the other passengers from the flight.

While pushing her cart towards the taxi rank she heard someone call out her name. Surprised, she turned and found herself staring into a pair of mesmerizing blue eyes, belonging to a very attractive man. He was about five inches taller than her and she guessed he was of a similar age. Going by the lack of recognition on her face, he realised she didn't have a clue who he was.

"It's Sean."

She looked confused and he tried again.

"Don't you remember me? I'm Sean…Sean Riley."

Her mind raced quickly, trying to remember him. Then it clicked. Could this attractive man be the same Sean Riley she had grown up with, the one who was constantly tagging along after her when she was a child? Annie remembered him as skinny and pimply-faced. Surely this couldn't be the same person? This handsome stranger bore no resemblance to *that* awkward boy.

He gently took her hand in his and she could feel his eyes devouring every inch of her face and body. She realised he was just as pleased as she was with the grown-up version. He leaned towards her and kissed her gently on both cheeks. The touch of his lips on her skin made her heart beat faster and she blushed…but he didn't seem to notice.

"I've come to take you home; I couldn't let you take a taxi."

She couldn't help but notice his soft Irish brogue.

"I'm so sorry for your troubles. Your daddy was a grand man and a good friend of mine; he will be sorely missed."

Her eyes started to fill with tears as she nodded in agreement, then Sean confidently took hold of her suitcases and left the cart behind. Together they crossed the street to the airport car park.

It was packed with cars of every shape and size, but he stopped by an older-type bright red Jaguar Roadster. It looked in mint condition. Annie was impressed with the car and wondered what he did for a living. He opened the door for her and she settled herself on the comfortable cream leather seat while he put her luggage in the boot and got in beside her.

It was as if he could read her mind.

"You know Annie," he said affectionately, "I took your advice."

She turned towards him.

"What advice was that? I don't remember giving you any advice?"

He smiled.

"Well, do you remember what a dunce I was in school; I was totally hopeless at Maths and English. Don't you remember that night in the park?"

She shook her head.

"No."

He looked disappointed that she didn't remember such an important time in his life, but continued with the recollection.

"I had just dismally failed all my exams and was sick with worry."

She thought back, but couldn't remember and answered him truthfully.

"I'm afraid I don't remember, Sean. It was a long time ago."

He studied her beautiful face, hurt that she couldn't recall the night that had changed his life.

"You told me not to worry about the things I couldn't do. Just concentrate on what I was good at. You told me to use my talents and that's what I did."

She looked at him questioningly.

"Don't you remember how much I loved music when we were kids? Well, that's what I do now for a living. I write songs and play guitar. You might have heard of us, I'm the lead singer with *The Turfs*. I put the band together with a few of the lads when all of us were virtually kicked out of school."

Annie was surprised. She not only knew who they were but also loved their music and had even bought some of their tapes and CDs. But, in her wildest dreams, she would never have associated the band with the Sean Riley she knew as a boy.

She studied him now with new respect. He was dressed beautifully in a stylish cream-coloured Nehru jacket over a black silk shirt and matching black wool trousers. She noticed the way his jet-black hair curled into the nape of his neck and she wanted to reach over and touch it.

She shook the thought away, feeling foolish.

"Did Daddy suffer much?"

She sounded despondent and he reached for her hand.

"No, it was all very sudden. He had his tea, said he was tired and went upstairs to take a nap. About an hour later, when your mother went to wake him, she found he had died in his sleep."

Annie felt needy and snuggled closer to him. He smiled and placed his left hand over hers. She could feel the warmth of his body surging through her, as if he were giving her the strength to carry on.

"I'm so relieved," she replied. "He was so afraid of dying from a lingering illness."

She noticed old familiar signs as they took the N11 towards Dublin. And she realized that the closer they got to her home, the more insecure she began to feel. Maybe it was because she would never see her father again. She tried to shake the negative feelings away. She must be strong for her mother.

When they arrived at the front of her mother's house, Annie got out of the car and walked slowly towards the front door, while Sean drove around to the back of the house to park. She was going to ring the doorbell, but changed her mind and decided to wait for him to return. Surprised, she recognized that she didn't want to go into the house by herself.

What was the matter with her? She was acting like a child. How many years would it take before she felt comfortable around her own mother? She reached for the bell, but her mother must have been watching for her and the door opened before she could ring it.

They greeted each other tearfully on the outside steps with Mary allowing a very restrained hug from her daughter. Annie noticed that her mother's eyes were red and puffy from crying.

"How am I going to live without him? He had no right leaving me alone, we were supposed to go together."

They went inside and Annie tried her best to console her mother. Then her younger sister and brother arrived at the house and rang the bell. The door was thrown open for them and they were kissed and hugged by her mother. Sean was standing behind them and he followed them inside.

Annie's younger sister Emily grabbed her and hugged her; then it was Derek's turn. He held his elder sister at arms length and studied her face.

"Good God, Annie, you've turned into a raving beauty. What happened to the ugly redhead who left home to make her fortune in London?"

He grinned, gave her a kiss and turned and slapped Sean on the back.

"Don't you agree, Sean, that my big sister's turned into a raving beauty?"

Sean smiled before responding.

"You know as well as I do that she was always a great beauty."

Annie could feel the blood rush to her face and turned away from his approving look, not wanting him to notice. She changed the subject and asked if she could see her father.

"I put him in your old bedroom," her mother replied.

"Derek, put Annie's things in the guest room and I'll go and make us a nice cup of tea."

And, without waiting for her daughter to respond, she headed towards the kitchen. Annie glanced at her brother who just shrugged, picked up her bags and headed for the stairs.

"She'll be OK. It's just the suddenness of his death. You know how close they were."

Emily was stroking the fox collar on Annie's coat.

"I love your coat. It's really beautiful. I'd love to have clothes like yours."

Annie looked affectionately at her and smiled. "You will, when you're older. I've brought you a present."

The girl's eyes lit up with excitement.

"What is it? Is it a dress? Is it jeans? Oh, *please* can I see it now?"

"I'll give it to you right after I see Daddy," Annie said, firmly, turning to head up the stairs.

Sean watched her go.

"Would you like me to come up with you?"

She shook her head.

"No thanks, I want to spend a few minutes alone with him."

As she climbed the narrow stairs to her old bedroom, she thought about the last time she'd seen her father. It had been a couple of months earlier, the day he took her to the airport for the flight to Milan; she was flying there for a photo shoot with Italian Vogue.

He had looked weary and a little sad when they said their goodbyes at the gate. He kissed her and held her in his arms just a little longer than usual. She had noticed tears in his eyes when he finally let her go and wondered if he had somehow sensed this was the last time they would be together.

Annie opened the door to the small bedroom that she used as a child. Her father was lying on the single bed, wearing his best navy suit. She was surprised that her mother hadn't used a funeral parlour. Surely no one laid people out at home anymore?

A large candle stood on each bedside table and their glow cast an unnatural, almost ghostly, light around the room. Her father looked as if he was asleep and might wake at any moment to give her one of his bear hugs.

Tears slid down her face as she studied him. She'd had so many plans for both her parents. Just a week ago she had arranged a surprise holiday for them in Paris. She would have to remember to cancel it, or maybe she could rearrange it so Emily and Mammy could go when the funeral was over; they would be ready for a holiday.

Why was she thinking about such trivial things at a time like this? Annie couldn't bear it and couldn't bring herself to stay in the room a moment longer; she left quickly, closing the door quietly behind her.

She could hear her mother moving about in the bedroom just down the hall, so she decided to join her.

She knocked timidly on the door, the way she had as a child (her mother had always insisted on having privacy). Her mother opened the bedroom door at once.

"Come in Annie, I was about to give you a call. I've got something for you."

Annie followed her into the room. It was still pale blue, with the same blue and yellow curtains she remembered as a child. It was as though time had stood still. Why hadn't her mother spent some of the money she sent her each week on some decorating? Or a new bed? The one she had looked old, lumpy and uncomfortable.

She glanced around her and once again she was a child, uncomfortable in her mother's presence. Annie felt weak with emotion and let her body sink into the chintz chaise-lounge. She studied her mother who was rummaging through the drawers by the side of the bed. She looked exhausted and was shocked at how stooped she had become. It seemed as if, overnight, her mother had turned into an old woman.

She had always been athletic and full of energy. What had happened to change her? It couldn't be the death of her father; the changes she saw in her mother didn't happen overnight. Annie decided that, as soon as the funeral was over, she would insist they visit a health spa together. Her mother was only in her fifties, still a young woman; she couldn't let her give up on life.

"Now where on earth did he put that dam letter?" her mother muttered.

"I know it was in this drawer—oh, here it is."

She pulled out a large manila envelope and handed it to Annie.

"It's from your father," she said coldly.

"He asked that you read it alone. I'll be downstairs, if you need me."

And, with that, she turned and left the room, leaving her daughter holding the mysterious envelope.

Annie studied it. What was so secretive that he couldn't share it with her mother? She carefully tore it open and removed two thin sheets of paper. A photograph fluttered to the ground. Annie picked it up and studied it. The paper was now yellow with age.

There were three people in the picture all dressed in tennis clothes. They were smiling happily at the camera and their rackets were on the ground next to their feet.

One of the men was obviously her father when he was a lot younger. His arm was around a pretty young girl in the middle of the photograph. She was more than pretty. She was beautiful. Annie noticed that she was taller than her father, smiling at him lovingly with her arm around his waist. Another young man stood next to them.

She turned the picture over and read: 'Jacqueline, Tim and me at the tennis club, 1978.'

Then her mind turned to the letter.

My darling Annie,

If you are reading this letter I will have passed on. I'm sorry I could never drum up the courage to tell you in person what you are about to learn. I know it will be a terrible shock to you. Please believe me when I say that I love you with all my heart and, if there were any way I could spare you this pain, I would.

Mary and I separated two years before you were born and I moved to Galway where Tim O'Shea and I set up a tennis club. I was the tennis pro and did most of the teaching and Tim took care of our accounts. A few months later a young girl joined our club, the girl in the picture. Her name was Jacqueline Ryan and she and I became intimately involved. I thought she was the loveliest most exciting woman I had ever known and we fell in love. I know it was wrong to get involved with her, she was only sixteen at the time and I was twenty-eight.

I'm ashamed to say that I couldn't keep away from her. We were soul mates and she was such a joy to be with. We met regularly over a six-month period and were gloriously happy.

Then one day she told me she was pregnant. She looked so happy and excited when she gave me the news about the baby, but I was stunned. How could she be pregnant? She was little more than a child herself and I had always been so careful with her and used protection whenever we made love.

She waited for my reaction and all I could think about was that she was underage and I was in deep trouble. Her parents were furious with her when they found out and they threatened me with prison.

I was beyond caring and, a few months later, I discovered where they had sent her to have our baby. You were that baby, Annie.

She had just turned seventeen when she wrote to me from the home. It was decided that, after you were born *and the trouble had died down, we would leave Ireland and settle in England where I could get a divorce and we could be married.*

The time went by and I arranged for Tim O'Shea to meet her on the Aran Isles. He was the young man in the picture with us.

He was going to tell her of my plans. Something must have gone wrong because Tim was supposed to bring her to the ferry at Dun Laoghaire for our trip to England. I waited for hours, but they never appeared.

It was as if they had vanished into thin air. At first I thought Tim had run away with her; but later on I found out that Jackie's parents had somehow found out about our plans and I wondered if Tim was responsible and didn't want to show his face. I knew he had a crush on her.

You can imagine how I felt, thinking the worst of my friend, when, days later, his body was washed up on the seashore in Galway. I never heard what happened to Jacqueline. I think she must have drowned with him.

I'm ashamed to say that I panicked and, like a coward, didn't follow up on her. I was afraid I'd be in more trouble if I did. So, instead, I went running back to Mary.

After Jacqueline's death, your grandparents didn't want you and they put you up for adoption. Father Killeen was a friend of mine and he arranged for Mary and me to adopt you. At that time we were childless and Mary was desperate for a baby.

She forgave me my indiscretion and helped me raise you as our own. I hope you will someday learn to forgive me. You know you have always held a special place in my heart.

Not a day has gone by when I haven't wished I had done things differently. Try to forgive me for turning your life upside down.

Love Daddy

A tear dropped onto the last words of the paper and she wiped it clean; but she didn't try to stop the tears that ran down her cheeks. Just a couple of sheets of paper and an old photograph and her world had turned upside down. Her life would never be the same. Mary was not her mother and Derek and Emily were only her half-brother and sister. Nothing from her past was as she had imagined. Not only had she lost her father, she had also lost her mother and her whole family.

She couldn't understand how her father, an educated man, could ignore the law, making love to an underage girl and then getting her pregnant; and how could he be so sure that she died in the accident with his friend, Tim? Her father hadn't even bothered to check if her mother was really dead. Annie wasn't sure she could ever forgive his cowardice and realized how little she really knew about him.

She felt drained and all cried out, but knew she had to go downstairs and face her family. Then she remembered they were not really her family any more. She placed the letter and photograph carefully back into the envelope and slotted it into the pocket of her tweed suit. She went down the hall into the bathroom, washed her face and rubbed the smears of mascara from beneath her eyes. Then she went down to the kitchen.

Annie noticed that the large wooden dining table was set for tea and Sean and the rest of her family were already sitting around it. Was it her imagination or did they look at her as if she didn't belong? Her mind was playing tricks on her.

Feeling uncomfortable and insecure she decided to sit next to Sean. He took her hand in his and gently stroked it.

"Was it awful?" he asked, looking worried.

Her mother's eyes met hers as she lifted the teapot and poured out a cup of tea.

"Did you read Daddy's letter?"

Annie nodded.

"Yes."

Her mother looked concerned.

"Do you want to talk about it?"

There was a puzzled expression on Derek's face.

"What letter?"

He set his teacup down so abruptly that the tea slopped over onto the carefully ironed white lace tablecloth.

"He left us a letter?"

Before Annie could respond, his mother said quietly: "It was for Annie."

With that, Annie pulled the letter from her pocket and handed it to him.

"You might as well know what it says," she said sharply. "It says that I'm a bastard; I'm not really your sister, I'm only your half-sister."

They all stared back at her in stunned silence. Derek took the letter from her and read it to himself first. Then he read it out loud, leaving out the very last bit. He knew it would hurt his mother.

There was silence around the table when he finished. He folded the letter and handed it to Annie who put it back in her suit pocket.

Sean was the first person to regain his composure and break the silence. He put his arms around Annie and hugged her close.

"It doesn't matter who gave birth to you, you're still part of this family. Mary is still your mother, and Dermot and Emily are still your brother and sister."

But, as Annie eyes met her mother's, she knew that wasn't the case. Mary had always been jealous of her husband's relationship with her real mother and she had never really forgiven him or truly accepted his illegitimate child.

Now Annie understood why Mary had brushed her aside through the years whenever she tried to show her love and affection—and why Dermot and Emily were treated differently. Over those years, when she watched her mother display the love she felt for Emily and

Derek, she prayed that one day Mary might feel the same way about her. Now she understood why that would never happen.

In the past, when she was sad, she had always been able to talk to her father and he had given her the love and affection she craved. He had never disappointed her. Now she had lost him as well and, even if he were still alive, she knew she would never feel the same way about him again. Why hadn't he confided in her when she was a child? He should have told her about her mother. It was wrong to keep her in the dark.

The room was heavy with sadness and regret. Annie suddenly felt ill from the heavy atmosphere. She stood up carefully, afraid she might be sick, excused herself and left the kitchen. She looked pale and depressed.

"I'm all in," she said. "I think I'll go up to bed."

She turned to Sean.

"Thanks again Sean, for picking me up from the airport."

Emily interrupted her.

"What about my present? Can I have it now? You promised you'd give it to me after you saw Daddy."

Mary glared at her daughter.

"How can you be so thoughtless? You know your sister's exhausted and needs to rest and all you can think about is yourself and your present!"

"It's all right, I understand, Ma…" Annie said. "It's in the back bedroom. Go on up, I'll be there in a minute."

Sean got up to leave. He went to the front door and turned and studied her.

"I'll see you tomorrow Annie. Try to get some sleep."

Then he turned towards Mary.

"What time do you want me here tomorrow morning, Mrs O'Hanlon?"

"Nine-thirty would be grand, Sean," Mary replied.

He glanced back at Annie, who was standing by the stairs watching him. She looked so tired and vulnerable, he wanted to hold her and make it all better. Emily had already raced upstairs ahead of her.

"Sean, I…" Annie stopped in mid-sentence.

He thought how pale and lovely she looked and had to force his arms against his sides to prevent himself from racing over to her and taking her in his arms.

"I'm a pallbearer with Dermot in the morning, along with two of the other lads from the band," he explained softly.

She nodded and moved from the stairs towards him. She was in front of him now and reached up to kiss him gently on the cheek. Her lips felt soft and, when she moved away, he looked surprised and unconsciously touched the place she had just kissed.

As she started back upstairs, Annie could hear Mary talking to him.

"We'll need you by 9.30 sharp, Sean, and remember to wear a dark suit."

CHAPTER 8

Edward Ryan was not a happy man. He had just finished his favourite meal of corned beef and cabbage, and his wife had picked at him through the entire dinner. He studied her critically; she was such a good-looking woman. If only she wasn't such a bloody pain in the arse. She loved to put him down and he was sick of her negative attitude and the way she interrogated him.

They had been married for over thirty years and she had always had the ability to make him feel insecure and a bloody idiot. And she was worse now that she was older.

She had turned into a controlling bitch. She loved talking down to him. He was a barrister and the head of a major law firm; and he had made her and her family a pot-load of money. Why couldn't she treat him with a little respect?

Her bossy know-it-all attitude had begun to irritate the hell out of him. He had only let her get away with it because she held the purse strings, something she never let him forget.

Elizabeth was an only child. She came from a wealthy family and liked to boast that her family had always had money, bringing it with them when they arrived in Ireland in Cromwell's time. But years ago Edward had checked her family line out and he knew better. There was nothing noble about her ancestors; they had been lowly immoral brigands in Cromwell's employ, taking the land she now owned by force from its original Irish owners.

Like her parent's before her, she made sure that the land and properties remained in her name. Her family gifted Edward 40 per cent of the shares, after he turned their company around. The law firm was on a fast track to the bankruptcy courts when he took over the management. Even then he had to fight for the shares he received. The old man hated the thought of Edward owning any part of his company. What Elizabeth's father couldn't stomach, was the idea that someone from a tenement in North Dublin had saved his firm from going under.

Edward also owned the house in Galway, bought and paid for with his own money. The rest of the land, made up of farms and commercial properties in Dublin, Cork and Galway, was in Elizabeth's name.

Years ago, Edward had realised that his wife's wealth and social standing in the community was more important to her than him or their family.

That was the day he took a mistress. Her name was Kathy Bourke and he had known her from the time he was a boy; she was the exact opposite of his wife. Kathy was full of love and passionate about him. When he was with her he felt happy. She had loved him from the time they were children. She was widowed now, having married a Dublin man a few years after he married Elizabeth. They had no children.

The affair with Kathy had picked up where it left off thirty years ago when Edward bumped into her at a Brown Thomas store. She worked in the card department and he had stopped in to buy a card for his secretary. Kathy had never forgotten Edward; he had been her first love and Edward was desperate for a little affection.

Edward studied his wife and wondered if she suspected there was someone else in his life?

Elizabeth was now in her early sixties, but looked ten years younger. She spent a good deal of money on her appearance and, like her husband, dressed stylishly in expensive designer suits.

Edward's childhood was totally different from his wife's. He grew up in North Dublin and was one of six children. His mother, who he adored, had been pregnant with ten, but endured two miscarriages and having two still—born. Edward was fifteen when his mother suffered one of her miscarriages. He had just come home from school and found her on her knees scrubbing the floor when he came home from school. The back of her dress was covered in blood and when he saw it he panicked. She begged him not to call a doctor, saying they couldn't afford the expense. She was haemorrhaging and he put her to bed and called for a doctor. That call saved his mother's life. He remembered his mother's soft voice and gentle dignity and the way she had loved her children and put them first.

He realised at a very early age that hard work was the only way out of the tenement they lived in. He had always been ambitious and worked from the time he was a little boy, running back and forth to the turf accountants on the corner of his street for a number of elderly housebound men and women. On weekends he was a newspaper boy and the money he earned helped feed their family.

Edward remembered his father with nothing but disgust. He was a useless drunk who never worked a day in his life, often beating his wife when he was drunk.

Edward was ten when he died and was not sorry. His father died the way he had lived, drunk as a lord. A car hit him as he weaved his way unsteadily across the road, heading for home. His son felt it was a fitting end to a wasted life.

Because of what he'd experienced at home, Edward always strived to better himself. He dearly loved his mother and was devastated when she died. He felt she was the only woman who had ever really understood or appreciated him. She was only forty-five when she died but looked like an old woman, her body worn out from giving birth to almost a football team of children and the abuse she suffered at the hands of her husband. There was also the stress of always having too little money to take care of her family.

Edward was twenty years old at the time, working as a builder's mate in the evenings and at weekends, to help pay his way through the law school he had won a scholarship to. He was heartbroken when he lost his mother; why couldn't the good Lord have let her live to see what he had accomplished with his life? He would have bought her a new house and treated her like a queen. Her memory was always with him, though, and he thought about her whenever he was troubled or needed affection. He knew in his heart that he had been her favourite. He expected the women he fell in love with to be like his mother; a loving, caring person.

He was twenty-six when he first met Elizabeth. She was already engaged to Tom McBride, when they met. It didn't take her long to dump her weedy-looking fiancé after she met Edward, who was then a trainee solicitor. He found out early on that she enjoyed 'a bit of rough' and he believed in accommodating her.

Now, Elizabeth regretted the mad passion she had felt towards him when they were young. Her sexual appetite had influenced her decision to say "Yes" when he asked her to marry him. In a way she also married Edward to punish her parents.

They had her life neatly arranged for her by the time she turned twenty. She was supposed to marry their best friend's son. Tom McBride's family was extremely wealthy and the marriage would mean an influx of money for Elizabeth's family. The money was desperately needed if they wanted to save their law firm.

She was open to the marriage, until she got engaged to Tom, and decided to test the goods. After she slept with him a couple of times, she found him wanting in the sex department and a dull and boring lover. There was no way she could bring herself to marry him, no matter what her parents thought.

Her father nearly passed out when she told him she was seeing Edward. He couldn't believe she would lower herself with someone from the wrong side of the tracks.

Elizabeth felt differently. Edward was a gorgeous looking man and a wonderful lover. There were a lot of other women waiting in the wings who had more than a passing interest in him. And he had a good head for business. She was afraid she might lose him to someone else if she didn't marry him right away.

The passion she felt for him long ago no longer existed, though. She couldn't even remember the last time they had slept together, or she had felt the slightest bit amorous in his company.

They moved into the parlour and she sat on the elegant Queen Anne chair next to the fireplace. Edward poured two glasses of sherry, handed her one and sat across from her. He wriggled uncomfortably in his chair; it was way too small for him. He hated the way she had furnished their home. The place reminded him of a bloody museum. Every damn piece of furniture was either ugly or hard and uncomfortable. *He hated bloody antique furniture.*

Elizabeth studied her husband's still handsome face. She knew he was angry with her and watched carefully for his reactions to her questions.

"What happened when you told the reporter he was wrong? When you said it was all a lie?"

Edward was not happy with the turn her questions had taken and responded angrily.

"Nothing happened, he believed me. Why can't you give me some credit? I know what I'm doing...just leave things alone.

Elizabeth shook her head.

"I can't leave things alone, Edward, because I don't feel you were right treating the reporter the way you did."

Edward face flushed with anger; *he should never have told her that he lost his temper with the reporter.*

You just love to pick holes in everything I do. I told you, he was a young insignificant little weasel, not worth worrying about."

He moved uncomfortably in the chair, knowing she didn't believe him. He tried again.

"Why do you have to pick holes in everything I do? Why can't you ever leave things alone? I've told you what happened," he said spitefully.

"I said she drowned with Tim O'Shea off 'Inish Mann'..."

Elizabeth knew what her husband could be like if she pushed him too far. He had a short fuse but she had to ask.

"And did he believe you?"

Edward's face flushed a deeper red and contorted with rage.

"Why the hell shouldn't he believe me? Of course he believed me. There's nothing to worry about."

Now *she* was angry.

"How can you be so sure? What if he decides to go ahead and print what you said about her death? What happens then? What if someone comes forward and decides to blackmail us?

Now he looked worried, but still wanted to control the conversation.

"Why would anyone want to blackmail us?"

She shook her head in disbelief.

"Stop hiding your head in the sand, Edward. You know there are people out there who would love to destroy us and the business."

Edward shook his head.

"And why would they want to do that?"

With a look of disgust she continued her verbal attack.

"Are you blind; surely you know you've made a lot of enemies over the years?

Then she got up and moved away from him.

"The problem with you, Edward, is you don't think of the consequences of your actions. You can't control your temper and mess things up. Your stupidity could cost us the business and possibly our freedom."

CHAPTER 9

Later the following morning, when the funeral at Glasnevin Cemetery was over, Mary had assumed that Annie would come home with them and join the family for a spread. Annie couldn't bring herself to go home. She explained to her stepmother, as politely as she could, that she would see them all later. Her feelings and emotions about her father and stepmother were all mixed up in her head. At the moment she didn't know how she felt about either of them.

She was having a hard time coming to terms with the thought that her father had lived a lie for twenty-five years. Why hadn't he come out with it and told her about her mother before? If she'd known sooner she could have checked things out for both of them.

What if her mother *was* still alive? But, if she were, surely she would have contacted Annie's father, or at least tried to see her own daughter?

Her mind was filled with unanswered questions as she drove with Sean to the pub on Doyle's Corner for a drink. They found a convenient parking space near by, went in and settled themselves at a quiet table in a corner of the pub.

The barman ambled over to serve them. He recognized Sean and asked him for his autograph. Sean responded graciously and the barman said the drinks were on the house, returning minutes later with two beers and a gracious smile. Another customer had come in and he went back behind the bar to serve him.

Sean studied Annie's face, noticing the dark circles under her eyes.

"I didn't think you were going to make it through the service," he said, concerned. "You looked so tired."

She rubbed her index finger over the moisture on the side of her beer glass and looked at him thoughtfully.

"I felt as if I shouldn't be there. It's like I'm no longer part of the family. I didn't sleep at all last night; I was thinking about Daddy and the letter he wrote to me. Why didn't he have the guts to tell me in person? He's made me feel like an outsider. It's as if I've lost them all, not just him."

Sean shook his head sympathetically.

"You've got to stop thinking that way. You know they all love you. So what if Mary's not your biological mother? She raised you, didn't she? And a darn good job she made of it."

"You don't understand, Sean. I have to find out about my real mother.

"I want to know everything about her; I have to know what she was like and what happened to her after I was born."

Sean leaned towards her. He looked worried.

"Do you really think that's such a good idea? How do you think Mary will feel if you go searching for Jacqueline?"

He had to stop her from any more hurt, stop her torturing herself.

"Remember, Mary was the person who was always there for you, not some 16-year-old girl."

But Annie wasn't listening.

"I've made up my mind. I'm going to find out everything I can about my mother. And I'd like you to help me, Sean. You're more familiar with Ireland than I am now—but if you don't want to get involved, I'll understand."

He could see she was determined to do it her way, but he had to try to save her from even more heartbreak.

"Have you thought of how much time the search could take? Remember, it all happened twenty five years ago."

She looked down at the table and traced her index finger again through the small pool of water left by her glass.

No, Sean, it didn't happen to me twenty-five years ago; it happened yesterday and, since then, I've thought about nothing else.

Sean took her hand.

"Can you take that much time off from your work?"

He could see she was trying to fight back the tears. She looked worn out and seeing her that way broke his heart.

I've already contacted my agent in London and told her I'll be staying in Ireland for another month or so to handle a family matter. She knows about my father's death, so she understands. And I've asked Terri to look after the cosmetics side of my business, while I'm here."

"Well, it looks like you've thought of everything," Sean replied, downing what was left of his beer. As she stood up to leave, he picked up her coat and held it open for her. He took pleasure in the delicate fragrance of her body as he helped her slip it on. He longed to take her in his arms, to kiss that lovely mouth and show her how much he loved her, how much he'd always loved her. But he felt she had enough to deal with at the moment.

"I'll help you find out everything I can about your mother," he said. "And we can start by visiting your biological grandparents. I'll do a bit of checking and find out where they live. And when we meet, they can fill us in on what happened to your mother. "

CHAPTER 10

When Sean arrived at Annie's house the following morning, she was already waiting outside with her overnight bag beside her. They had planned on being away two nights in Galway, as Sean had a gig there with his band. He took the holdall from her and placed it next to his in the boot of the car. They settled themselves in and then set off for the motorway that would take them to Galway.

The day before, Sean had checked on Annie's grandparents and discovered that they had been living in Galway for a long time, so he felt there was a reasonable chance their granddaughter was born in the area. He felt their best chance of learning anything at all about her mother was through her grandparents.

As they drove towards Galway, Sean didn't have the heart to tell her that he'd already spoken to her grandfather on the telephone, and it wasn't a happy call.

The man appeared to be an extremely rude individual, refusing to answer the majority of his questions and Sean thought he sounded panic-stricken when he told him his granddaughter wanted to visit him to enquire about her mother.

He had told Sean to tell her to forget it; he and his wife didn't want to meet her, they wanted nothing to do with her. Then the telephone had gone dead.

But Sean was no quitter and he decided that, regardless of what her grandfather felt, Annie should meet them both face-to-face. He was sure that when they met their lovely granddaughter they would soften towards her.

As they drove westward, they chatted about everything under the sun. They were surprised at how relaxed they felt in each other's company. Sean told her about some of the weird and wonderful things he experienced in his early days with the group. One club was so rough that the owners had fitted wire netting in front of the stage to prevent bands getting bombarded by flying beer bottles.

She laughed at his story of the band playing in a rural village hall, situated just across the road from the churchyard. Their bass player, Dave, chatted up a local girl whenever they were not actually playing, and she wanted to take him across the road to make passionate love to him amongst the gravestones. Dave turned down the offer, he chickened out. He didn't like the idea of ending the night with 'Rest in Peace' impressed on his back.

Annie told Sean about her life as a model and some of the humorous things she had experienced. She let him know what some of those innocent looking young models were capable of when they felt you were competition.

There was the big runway show in Paris when another model had deliberately given her a hard push on the back as she started out down the runway. Annie was wearing sandals with four-inch heels and it was impossible to control the momentum as she shot down the catwalk. Two other models were already in the centre of the runway and they watched in horror as she flew towards them. The collision knocked all three of them off their feet and they tumbled off the catwalk, landing on top of a group of very surprised but delighted young men seated in the front row.

Sean threw his head back and roared with laughter, almost steering them off the road and into a ditch.

Annie loved how his face lit up and his mouth crinkled at the corners when he laughed. She had read somewhere that men with a strong sense of humour were good in bed, and she wondered if that were true of Sean. It was a long time since she had had such feelings for a man.

Nick was the last man she had felt anything for; he was appropriately named as he turned out to be a cheater and a loser, like his namesake. She was with him for two years and they planned to be married the following April. Nick was living with her at her apartment in Mayfair. She was away a lot on modelling assignments, so he usually had the apartment to himself.

It was at the end of their second year together. It was Christmas Eve and Annie returned home early that day, to surprise him. She had shopped before heading home and she was loaded down with gifts for him.

She opened the front door quietly as she wanted to surprise him. He wasn't in the living room and she heard music coming from the bedroom; he must have gone to bed early, so she decided to join him. She pushed the door open with her foot, intending to cover him with his gifts.

She was the one who got the surprise; she found Nick was already covered, but it was with a young sexy blonde model. She recognised the girl, she had worked with her a few times.

Annie must have looked stunned and the young girl smirked in satisfaction when she saw how upset she had made her competition. She had always been jealous of Annie and her success, this would show her.

She took great delight in letting Annie know that she and Nick had been an item and had slept together regularly when she was away.

Nick looked worried as Annie's stunned expression turned to bitter anger. He had to try and save the fancy lifestyle he had become accustomed to with her. He tried to weasel his way out of things. The girl had meant nothing to him; she was just a bit on the side. Sex with her wasn't better it was just different.

Annie told him what he could do with his bit of different as she threw her engagement ring in his face.

"Get the hell out of my life."

Then he tried one last desperate attempt to sort things out, saying: "She didn't man anything to me, she seduced me…it was her fault."

When the model heard what he said, she screamed at him: "You bastard," and attacked him with her nails. He tried hiding under the sheets to get away from the assault as the girl went crazy.

"You were the one who went after me, you told me that Annie was just a friend who kept some of her clothes here, when she was away.

Nick was trying to get dressed as the young model continued to scream at him.

You lied to me, you bastard, you used me."

Annie was disgusted with the two of them and told them that if they weren't dressed and out of her apartment in the next few minutes she was calling the police.

She gave Nick fifteen minutes to take everything he owned, along with the unhappy model, and leave. She couldn't believe his nerve when he asked if he could take his Christmas presents with him. His girlfriend looked surprised when she found out that Annie owned the apartment, not Nick.

Annie wondered later how many other women had shared her bed with him while she was away? And she made a note to get rid of the bed and get a new one the next day.

After that dreadful experience she had a hard time trusting men and was extra careful not to get involved. She concentrated solely on her work. The relationship with Nick turned her off men in general.

Terri was her roommate now. It was two years since she broke up with Nick.

She smiled as she thought of the name the other models had given her. They called her 'The Ice Queen'.

She wondered what they would say, if they knew what she was thinking about this lovely man sitting next to her, at this very minute. And the exciting thoughts that kept running through her head; what would he be like in bed? She visualised how he would look naked, imagining him to be a thoughtful and caring lover.

Sean moved closer and she felt her heart skip a beat. Did he know what she was thinking? Embarrassed, she shook herself free of her disturbing flight of fancy. They were on a mission and, for the moment, she had no time for romantic entanglements no matter how much they appealed to her. She kept reminding herself what had happened with Nick; she couldn't afford another disappointment.

She returned to the problem of her father and stepmother.

"You know, Sean, I think I've always known deep down that Mary was not my real mother. She was always so reserved around me. As a child I used to long for her love and approval but she never really showed me any real affection. I guess she never really loved me," she said sadly.

Sean looked surprised.

"I had no idea that things were that bad at home," he replied, trying to keep his eyes on the road but stealing a glance in Annie's direction.

As children they had been the best of friends, telling each other their most intimate secrets; but he still hadn't recognized that she was having problems at home. He should have listened and questioned her more. He should have made her tell him what was bothering her. Growing up could be painful in the best of families.

He remembered the year he turned thirteen. He grew six inches that year and ended up towering over his Irish friends. And, as if that weren't bad enough, his face and shoulders were plagued with acne. It was so embarrassing. His chin was covered in red pimples with little yellow heads; he looked disgusting and his back was even worse, it being covered in purple-looking welts.

Annie was the only person who seemed to understand how he felt. Unlike him, she was a lovely child with her delicate oval face and large hazel eyes. She was tall for a girl but he liked that. After all, he was six-foot-four himself.

He recalled the way they used to meet in the old coal shed at the bottom of her garden to talk and play games when they were kids. Checkers was a popular game along with Chess and a lot of times he knew she let him win. Even as a child she was good for his ego. Only now did he realise how very lonely she had been. And she wasn't alone, as far as being unhappy and lonely were concerned. They had both experienced those feelings at that time in their lives.

He would never forget the day she turned seventeen; she looked so beautiful. A week before her birthday, he had gone to Molly Flanagan's bakery to order a special cake from her. Molly had suggested two red hearts and some pink roses, and kidded him about his new girlfriend. He was thrilled that she might imagine that Annie could be interested in him.

When he collected the cake, he found that Molly had written 'Happy Birthday Annie, Love Sean', across the top. It was packed in a big cardboard box, along with seventeen candles.

When he arrived at Annie's house, with the cake, he found her alone. He handed her the box and, when she opened it and saw the cake, she looked surprised and happy at the same time. She went into the kitchen to get a knife and two plates. Sean followed her, fantasizing about what would happen when she blew out the candles.

He could picture her in his arms as he confessed his undying love for her.

She placed the cake on a fancy cake stand on the kitchen table and set out plates for each of them. Then she arranged the candles on the cake and lit them; laughing about being careful or she might burn the house down. Then she closed her eyes, blew out the candles and made a wish.

He watched her. She was so beautiful and he prayed that she was wishing he would kiss her—but she wasn't. Instead she blurted out: "Sean…" and her eyes shone with excitement. "I'm moving to England…I'm going to become a model. One of the biggest agents in London has sent me a contract and they've guaranteed, well promised me, a lot of money."

Sean couldn't believe his ears; his world collapsed around him. He doubled up as if someone had punched him in the stomach. He couldn't stand the thought of her leaving him. His heart was broken in two. The girl he loved was going away, she was leaving him. He felt physically ill and couldn't catch his breath.

Panicked, he tried to suck in a mouthful of air but nothing happened. He was suffocating, he couldn't breathe. He fell to the floor, his heart pounding so fast he thought it would burst. Annie raced to the kitchen and came back with a paper bag. She told him to breathe into it. It took just a few minutes that seemed like hours; but it worked. Then he felt embarrassed about what had happened—he felt like he wanted to die.

He wished the floor would open up and swallow him. He felt such a wimp. Somehow he covered up his feelings, babbling that he was coming down with the flu, and he heard himself saying how happy he was about her good fortune. He even wrote a song for her later that day. She had always remained in his thoughts and heart.

She promised he could visit her when she got a place of her own, but he hadn't taken her up on the offer. His band played dozens of dance halls and clubs in and around London where she lived, and he could have called her a dozen times during the years that followed. Perhaps he should have called, but he held back; she was so desirable and visible.

Her image was everywhere. He saw her on billboards, on the covers of magazines, on television interviews. It seemed she was constantly in the news, pictured at some elaborate party or other, and there was invariably a handsome young man at her side. He couldn't face a second rejection and the thought of her with another man. But now, here she was, back in Ireland—and they were together again.

Maybe this time things would turn out the way he wanted. She was a sexy, desirable woman now, but still the same lovely girl he remembered from his childhood.

However, he couldn't afford to be hurt again. This time he would take things slowly and, if she rejected him again, he would have to find a way to forget about her.

His thoughts returned to the present and he heard her say angrily: "Why didn't my father trust me enough to tell me about my real mother when he was alive? I'll never forgive him for not letting me know."

"I'm sure he didn't mean to make you suffer," Sean replied.

"I know he loved you with all his heart and, from what I read in his letter, he loved your real mother a lot as well."

Annie's eyes filled with tears.

"But, because of him, Mary never really accepted me as her daughter and it ruined my childhood."

He felt her pain and saw tears in her eyes again.

"I thought I wasn't lovable enough. But, all the time, it was because she couldn't bring herself to look at me. Or to accept me. I was a constant reminder of his affair; how could he expect her to accept his bastard child? How could he make me suffer like that?"

Sean pulled the car over to the side of the road and, without saying a word, took her in his arms and held her close to his heart. Her face was wet against his face and he kissed the tears away, then his mouth sought hers, and his kiss was gentle and caring.

She responded and then the kiss changed for Sean. It was filled with years of loving her and wanting her. And she didn't pull away. Surprisingly she returned his kiss with the same passion that he felt. When they did finally pull apart, both of them were shaken by the surge of emotion they experienced during the embrace and they sat side by side, not saying a word.

Sean restarted the engine, but his mind was racing. What had just happened? Did she feel the same way he felt about her? She had returned his kiss with such feeling, but what if it meant nothing to her? What if it was just the emotions of the moment? He had to be sure…he didn't want to force himself on her. He wanted her to love him for himself and not because she felt some duty towards him.

Not just because she felt beholding to him, because he was helping her out during one of the roughest periods of her life.

Annie didn't know what to think. She was just as shocked as Sean, at the feelings that his passionate kiss had stirred in her. She wanted him to love her but her mind told her to *take it slow*, remember what happened with Nick.

'Stop…don't get involved with anyone at the moment…it could destroy your relationship with Sean, if you got involved,' her mind was saying. She couldn't afford to lose his friendship. She would have to be careful around him and slow things down. They drove on into Galway, both locked in their own thoughts.

When they arrived at the Glenlo Abbey Hotel, he went to park the car while she went to reception to sign in and get the keys to their rooms. She noticed that the room numbers were next to each other and asked if she could change them; but the receptionist told her there was a film festival in town and the hotel was sold out—they were the only rooms available.

Sean approached, looking so handsome that her heart skipped a beat. He was still making his way towards her when he was stopped halfway by screams of delight coming from three pretty young women who had recognised him. They were obviously fans.

Annie watched jealously as they hung on his every word. One of them, a little older than the rest, was a very pretty blonde who kept touching his arm as he signed an autograph for her. Annie felt angry first with the girl, and then with Sean. In her heart she knew she was being unfair; it wasn't his fault that he was a celebrity. And the women were only getting an autograph. Why was she feeling jealous over a man she hadn't seen in eight years? What was wrong with her? She picked up their two small overnight bags and made her way to the lift. Sean excused himself from the girls and hurried after her.

Taking the bags from her, he said. "I'm sorry about that. You know how it is with fans; sometimes they materialize out of thin air."

She nodded her head in agreement.

As they arrived at her room he took the key from her, unlocked the door and placed her overnight bag on the floor inside. He asked if she'd like to have dinner later on but she declined, feigning tiredness. He looked disappointed.

"I'll see you in the morning then for breakfast. Shall we say about eight? I'd like to make an early start."

She nodded and quickly closed the door after him. The room she found herself in was a delight, one of the most romantic she had ever seen. Much of it was taken up with a canopied four-poster bed covered in cream and white lace. She smiled to herself, thinking she should have shot her commercial there. She noticed the adjoining door leading to Sean's room. Why had he picked this particular hotel?

She relived that sensual kiss they had shared by the side of the road and shivered. Was she falling in love with him? After watching TV for a while, she slept fitfully, wanting desperately to open the adjoining door and invite him in. But she stopped herself. This trip was not about her; it was about saying goodbye to Jacqueline, the woman who had given her life.

Sean knocked on her door promptly at eight the next morning ready for breakfast. She was ready too, casually dressed in a pair of snug-fitted rust-coloured suede jeans, high boots, and a long cream crewneck sweater. Her long auburn hair hung in loose waves around her shoulders and he told her how young and pretty she looked, not at all like a supermodel.

An hour later they arrived at her grandparents' house. It was behind high hedges, at the end of a long gravelled driveway. They parked in the designated parking area close to the elegant Georgian property.

Annie felt intimidated by it and said nervously: "I still think we should have called first." Sean felt uncomfortable too, still not having told her that he had spoken to her grandfather the day before. The man was not the least bit friendly. He was rude and insensitive and had nothing good to say about Annie or her father. Sean could only hope that, once he finally met his granddaughter, he would feel differently.

He rang the bell by the elaborate front door. The housekeeper opened it to them.

Annie spoke first.

"I'm Annie O'Hanlon and this is Sean Riley. We're here to see Mr and Mrs Ryan regarding their daughter Jacqueline."

The housekeeper told them that Mr. Ryan was away, but she would see if Mrs. Ryan was available. She invited them into the living room then left them alone.

Annie glanced nervously around the big room. Was that a picture of her mother on the wall? She moved towards it, her back towards the door as she studied the picture. Elizabeth Ryan entered the room and Annie turned quickly around. Her grandmother's hand flew to her mouth and she stared at the girl in shocked disbelief.

She whispered: "My God, it's Jacqueline…" before fainting and collapsing to the floor.

Annie bent over her grandmother. The housekeeper had been in the adjoining room when she heard the exclamation and rushed in, just in time to see her employer collapse.

"My God," she whispered putting her hand to her mouth. "What have you done? What happened? What did you say to her?" she exclaimed anxiously.

"I didn't say anything! She called me Jacqueline and then passed out."

The elderly housekeeper looked intensely at Annie. Yes, she could certainly see the resemblance; the young woman in front of her did look a lot like her darling Jacqueline.

Bridget had loved her charge from the day the child was born; loved her as if she were her own daughter. But, for now, she brushed aside thoughts of Jacqueline and rushed to the bathroom. She returned with a wet facecloth and placed it on the older woman's forehead. Why had her employer fainted at the sight of her visitor?

The older woman stirred and slowly sat up, still obviously light-headed. Annie and Sean tried to help her up to her feet but were brushed aside as she rose unsteadily from the floor on her own and flopped into the nearest chair.

She stared at them both for a few minutes, curiously, and then addressed Annie.

"Who are you? You couldn't be my daughter; she'd be much older now."

Then, with more control and in a commanding tone of voice, said: "Bridget, please bring me a brandy right away."

"I'm your granddaughter," Annie replied softly. "I'm Jacqueline's daughter."

The woman gestured towards Sean.

"This is Sean, he's my best friend. I grew up with him."

He leaned forward with an outstretched hand but she ignored him.

"I remember now," she said, her voice cold and unfeeling. She motioned towards Sean.

"You spoke to my husband yesterday."

She stared at him.

"I thought he made it quite clear that he wanted nothing to do with John O'Hanlon's daughter, so why did you bring *her* here?"

She pointed towards Annie.

"Did you really think I'd feel any differently than he did?"

Annie moved closer to Sean; there were tears in her eyes. He took her hand in his and stroked it, furious at the uncaring bitch sitting in front of him and by the way her cruel words had hurt Annie.

"I brought Annie to meet you. I felt sure that when you saw what a wonderful granddaughter you had, you would want to get to know her. Obviously I was wrong."

He looked disgusted as he stood up and turned his back on the woman.

But Elizabeth Ryan wasn't through yet.

"How can you expect me to be thrilled at the thought of meeting John O'Hanlon's daughter when you know that he was the one who killed my little girl?"

Annie was stunned at the direction the conversation had taken. This woman had just accused her father of killing her mother. She studied the woman closely. She didn't trust her. It was her turn to be angry now.

"I don't believe you. My father was a good man and he would never have killed the woman he loved."

Elizabeth stared back at her.

"I don't care whether you believe me or not. I tell you he killed her. Now kindly leave my house. Bridget, show them out this minute."

Sean turned towards Annie.

"Let's get out of here. She doesn't deserve you."

Bridget led them to the front door, slamming it shut behind them.

They walked towards the car in silence. Annie was close to tears and Sean was helping her into the car when Bridget showed up, as if from nowhere, standing next to them. She had obviously rushed round from the back of the house. She suggested they all meet at The Anchor pub in about half an hour; she had something important to tell them.

Bridget quickly left the way she had arrived, hoping her employer hadn't seen her.

CHAPTER 11

They soon found The Anchor pub and settled themselves at a table in one of the darker corners of the lounge. Sean was still at the bar getting their drinks when Bridget arrived and headed straight for their table. She bent towards the girl and gave her a hug.

"Me darling…You're so like your dear mother." Her accent was rich with Irish brogue and there were tears in her eyes.

Sean returned to the table carrying three pints of local ale. He handed one to Annie and one to Bridget.

"I hope this is OK?"

Bridget nodded. "Sure, that's grand."

She took a sip and then she smiled at Annie.

"I loved Jackie, that's what I called her. She was like my own sweet daughter. It was me who raised her, not those cold-blooded parents of hers."

Annie was taken aback by the woman's obvious love for her mother. Here, finally, was someone who had known her. She put her arms around Bridget and hugged her tightly.

"What was she like? What was my mother like?" she asked excitedly.

Bridget studied the young woman.

"Sure, she looked a lot like you. She was about your height and colouring but her hair was darker than yours. She was bright, really clever. When she was a child she wanted to become the first lady attorney to work in her daddy's office. And she loved you with all her heart, she was a wonderful mother."

Annie's mouth dropped open at what Bridget had just said.

"But I thought she…"

She tried again.

"Bridget, you said Jacqueline was a good mother but I was told that she died soon after I was born."

Bridget looked surprised.

"And where did you hear such a lie? Your mammy took care of you until you were two years old and a good mother she was too."

Annie wondered what was going on. In her father's letter, he had said that her mother died when she was a few months old. Now Bridget was telling her that her mother was still alive when she was two years old. Was her grandmother telling the truth? Had her father killed Jacqueline?

Sean was as surprised as she was.

"I don't understand," he said. "When did Jacqueline die?"

Bridget looked uncomfortable.

"It happened when Annie was two years old. I remember that awful day as though it were yesterday. Your mother asked me to look after you. She said she was going out but she would return later that night. She was so flushed and excited that I suspected she was meeting a young lad who meant a great deal to her. She told me she was going to Inish Mann, that's one of the Aran Isles."

Annie knew; she nodded as Bridget continued.

"That was the last time I ever saw her. Your grandparents said she fell over a cliff and drowned."

Her face was wet with tears just remembering, and Annie reached out for her hand.

"Then, against my wishes, Mr and Mrs Ryan put you up for adoption. I told them I could take care of you but they wouldn't hear of it. I could never understand how they could give up; their own flesh and blood?"

Bridget looked around her, hoping other people in the bar hadn't heard what she had been saying. She quickly finished her drink and made a move to leave.

"I have to get back to the house. It's almost dinner time and they'll be missing me."

Annie suggested they exchange telephone numbers and keep in touch and Sean got up as the two ladies hugged and said goodbye.

CHAPTER 12

Annie and Sean ate a quick dinner in the early evening at a little local restaurant. There was little time to discuss the events of the day, as he had to leave to get to the Ardilaun House Hotel and be ready for his gig that evening.

He showed Annie where his band was going to be. There was a large stage in the elegant room where he would be performing. The room was already filled to capacity. Annie guessed that it seated about 400 people. It appeared to her, sitting near the back, that the cream of Irish society was here. The seminar earlier in the day had been well attended and it seemed most of the people had stayed behind after the seminar to enjoy the entertainment.

Annie wore her hair up and an elegant off-the-shoulder red velvet dress that showed off her colouring to perfection. She was glad she had remembered to bring the dress with her to Galway. It was long and pleasing to the eye and clung to her body in all the right places. She had accessorized it with her good pearl choker necklace and pearl earrings. She knew that the dress gave out the right message and offered elegance, with a hint of sex appeal.

There was a tremendous round of applause from the audience as Sean and the band made their way up on stage. Annie thought they looked very trendy in their black leather trousers and waistcoats. She was pleasantly surprised as she watched Sean introduce the band. She hadn't known what to expect. Somehow she hadn't expected him to be so at home on stage and convey so much charisma. And when he started to sing she realised he also possessed a very good singing voice and was an excellent guitarist. No wonder the female fans at the hotel were mad about him.

After about the fourth song the audience started yelling out their favourites. Someone yelled: "Sing Annie's song…Sean…please…we want Annie's song!"

Sean looked uncomfortable at first, and he spoke so softly that she had to strain to hear him.

"Annie's song was the first song I ever wrote. I was seventeen at the time and I wrote it for my first love."

Then, as if drumming up his courage, he said in a louder voice: "The lady I wrote the song for is here tonight."

His voice broke slightly as he added: "Annie, this is your song…this song's for you."

Annie blushed, feeling embarrassed as four hundred pairs of eyes turned towards her. She couldn't believe that the young lad she had known since she was a child was actually going to play a song he had written about her all those years ago.

The song was all about her seventeenth birthday and it made her realise how much he had loved her and how callous she must have seemed when she told him about her modelling contract. She wondered if he still felt the same way about her, or was he as afraid of getting involved as she was? As she watched him perform the song with so much feeling, she realised that it was too late. She was already half in love with him.

When the song was over the applause was deafening and the band received a standing ovation.

Later that night, after it was all over, they walked hand in hand under the silver stars through the city of Galway, enjoying just being together. It was after midnight when they returned to the Glenlo Abbey. Annie was surprised that she already felt so comfortable around him.

They walked down the hallway and, when they got to her door, he gave her a gentle goodnight kiss. Before he could move away she had wrapped her arms around his neck and kissed him back with an eagerness that surprised both of them. Thrilled, he responded eagerly with a longing and fervour from years of loving her and wanting her.

He took the key from her, pushed open the bedroom door with his foot and they tumbled into her bedroom, tearing at each other's clothes as they staggered towards the bed. In seconds they were naked and lying on the luxurious duvet.

Their lovemaking was filled with years of heat and passion. He kissed her and kissed her, touching the most sensual places of her body with the tip of his tongue as she thrilled to his lovemaking. They couldn't get enough of each other; she shuddered with excitement as he circled her nipples with his tongue. She ran her hands down his manly body discovering him. She had never wanted anyone as much as she wanted him at that moment. Their lovemaking was filled with years of need and yearning as they finally came together in a shuddering and noisy climax.

They lay in each other's arms and talked long into the night, making love again and again before falling into a deep contented sleep with his arms still around her.

The next morning they headed back towards Dublin, happy in the knowledge that they had found each other but disappointed that they hadn't learnt more about Annie's mother and how or when she died.

Sean left Annie at her mother's house; he was leaving for a week's tour of Britain and had begged her to come with him. Now that he'd found her he couldn't bear the thought of being away from her. Annie told him no, she felt she needed more time to sort out her relationship with her stepmother. There were so many questions she wanted to ask Mary and she was the only person who might have some of the answers.

She explained that, as much as she'd love to join him, she knew how hard it was to try and socialize when he was working. He was disappointed, but accepted her decision and said he'd call her from England; they'd do something special when he got home.

CHAPTER 13

Two days later, Dermot Moore, contacted Annie for the first time, explaining that he was a reporter from *The Star* newspaper and suggesting they should meet for a chat. He had some important information regarding her biological mother. He didn't tell her that the newspaper had fired him the week before. She agreed to meet him and they settled on a time and place for the following day.

The next day she arrived early at their agreed meeting place, Doyle's Corner pub. Jacqueline ordered a glass of red wine and waited anxiously at a corner table, wondering who Dermot Moore was, and what sort of information he had about her mother.

He arrived about five minutes later and scanned the room for a woman sitting on her own and saw Annie. Sensing he was the right person, she waved to him. He ordered a beer and joined her. He shook her hand; impressed by the way she looked.

"Hi, I'm Dermot, I hope you haven't been waiting long."

Annie shook her head, thinking: *'Get to the point, I'm sick of small talk'*. But saying: "You said you had some news for me regarding my mother Jacqueline."

"Yes," he replied. "That's correct."

He studied the young woman seated across from him. She was a real beauty with her masses of long red hair, a real Irish beauty. He couldn't help noticing how much she resembled her grandfather. She had his mouth and the same large hazel eyes and good posture. He knew what he was about to tell her would be a huge shock to her.

"I believe that your mother is still very much alive."

Annie was stunned and waited for him to continue. The young man had the appearance of someone down on his luck. Annie had met plenty like him in her work.

"What do you mean, she's alive?"

Was she being conned by this dishevelled looking man? She felt confused and angry. First her father had said that her mother died of natural causes and then her grandmother said that wasn't true and swore that Annie's father had murdered Jacqueline. Now this man was telling her that her mother was still alive. What was the truth?

"Haven't you heard that my mother is dead?" She asked angrily. "She died in an accident; she drowned."

She spat the words at him.

He studied her closely before blurting out a response.

"You're wrong. Your mother's locked away in a mental hospital."

She was stunned by what he said and it took her several seconds to cool down. Was he mad? How could her mother be in an institution? If that were true, surely her father would have known?

"How do you know the woman you are talking about is my mother? Have you actually met her and spoken to her?"

He took a large gulp of beer before answering.

"No...err...I haven't actually spoken to her yet or met her personally, but a contact of mine told me where we could find her."

Annie looked at him suspiciously.

"And who was this informant?"

She was getting really mad now.

"And how do you know he or she was telling you the truth, if you haven't even bothered to follow it up and meet the woman for yourself?"

She wasn't going to buy it. He would have to convince her, make her believe him. He studied her thoughtfully.

"He's been right in the past and, if Jacqueline was supposed to have drowned, how come they never found her body?"

"But…" Annie replied suspiciously. "My own grandmother told me she was dead. Why would she lie about her daughter?"

At the mention of her grandmother, a look of disgust came over his face.

"If she's anything like her husband, she has to be bad news. So, if what she's saying is correct and your mother is dead, why did your grandfather attack me in his office?"

She looked surprised.

"He did what?" she asked.

"He tried to strangle me in his office when I told him what I had found out about his daughter."

He studied her face. Was he now getting through to her?

"Then he called my editor and tried to get me fired."

Dermot didn't mention that he had succeeded. If he did she might not believe any of his story.

She didn't look surprised by his comments. She remembered how her grandmother had treated her in Galway when she was questioned about her mother. And from what Bridget said, her grandfather was just as bad. *What if this man was right? What if her mother was still alive? If her grandmother had nothing to hide, why had she acted so strangely when she was questioned?* Her heart quickened at the thought of maybe finding her mother. And she realised that, for whatever reason, she did believe what this overweight young man was telling her.

That evening, when Sean called from England, she told him what had happened. He was astounded, saying that he had been suspicious all along and wondered what on earth was going on. The way her grandmother had reacted was odd to say the least. Why was she so anxious to get rid of them? And then there was the way she acted towards Annie, her own flesh and blood. It didn't make any sense. It just wasn't normal.

Annie felt a lot better listening to him. What he said made perfect sense. He felt the same as she did. They were definitely hiding something. Something strange was going on.

She told Sean that the journalist would be stopping by her house in the morning and they planned on driving to County Cork, where he'd been told they could find her mother. He believed she was now a resident in Rosemont Mental Hospital. If it were true, then the poor woman had spent the last twenty-five years of her life locked away there. She wondered if her mother was mentally ill. Then again, what if she was sane and had been locked up in an asylum all these years? The thought of something so dreadful happening to her mother was most alarming.

Before she hung up she checked that she had Sean's mobile phone number, promising she would contact him the moment she found out anything. Then, though hundreds of miles apart, they exchanged a goodbye kiss.

CHAPTER 14

When Dermot hadn't arrived on time the next morning, Annie's heart sank. Had he changed his mind? Maybe her father had been right, after all, and her mother had died in a boating accident. Then the telephone rang. Mary answered it and called to Annie.

"It's the Mater Hospital. They want to talk to you."

Annie was nervous as she took the receiver. A crisp voice on the other end of the line introduced herself as O'Toole, a nurse at the Mater Hospital.

"One of our patients, Dermot Moore, has asked me to call you. He was in a very serious accident last night. He'd like to see you but, due to the severity of his injuries, if you decide to visit it can only be for a few minutes. He is really too ill for visitors but he's in Ward Six."

Annie thanked her and the line went dead. The woman had hung up before Annie could ask what had happened to him.

Mary was still in the room and she noticed how shocked her stepdaughter looked. Should she ask her what was going on? Their relationship had deteriorated so much since Annie had come home for her father's funeral, she really didn't know how to speak to her daughter any more. She was worried about the girl.

In her own way she had always loved her adopted daughter. Without meaning to, it was her husband who had kept them apart. He had pushed her aside and almost raised Annie on his own; in the process, he had virtually ignored their two other children. She would never forgive him for that. He had left her no choice but to lavish all her love and attention on Annie's brother and sister.

"Why did the hospital call you? Is something wrong?" she asked.

"It's a friend of mine," Annie replied, very worried.

"He's a reporter and he's been in a bad accident. He was supposed to meet me this morning."

She really didn't want to go into the whole business with her stepmother.

"I've got to go to the hospital to see him."

She couldn't let Mary know that she and Dermot were on the point of tracking down her real mother. Mary had been hurt enough already. During the last few days Annie had put herself in her stepmother's shoes. She had gone through a similar situation with Nick and now she also appreciated how she would feel if Sean cheated on her, the way her father had on Mary.

From what she could tell he had never really gotten over Jacqueline. How could her stepmother possibly compete with a sixteen-year-old girl?

Mary had been deprived of her husband's love and affection for most of her married life. It must have hurt her deeply when she found out about the other woman in his life; and then to compound the situation, he had brought his love child into her home.

Tears of sympathy filled Annie's eyes, as she looked at Mary. She threw her arms around her stepmother and kissed her. This time Mary didn't push her daughter away; she held her close.

"There, there child," she said, patting her on the back. "Don't you fret yourself, child. Everything will be OK. Would you like me to come with you to the hospital?"

Annie shook her head, too choked with emotion to answer.

When she arrived at Ward Six there were ten beds in the room. All were occupied and most of them already had two or three visitors around them. Annie searched for Dermot and finally found him behind a curtain that circled his bed.

She was shocked when she saw his condition. He was covered in so many bandages that he looked like a mummy in a horror film. His head looked twice its normal size and he wore a full body cast. He saw her standing there and tried to force a smile, but his lower lip was split and he grimaced with the pain.

"My God, Dermot, what on earth happened to you?"

He mumbled something Annie couldn't make out, so she leaned in closer to him.

"Someone tried to kill me. The police want me to believe that it was a hit-and-run accident, but I know it was deliberate."

It seemed to hurt him to even take in a lungful of air. His breathing was shallow but he managed to keep talking.

"I must have been getting too close. I didn't want to tell you in case it might scare you, but someone's been following me since I left your grandfather's office. I think the same man followed me into the pub when we were there yesterday. I didn't want to mention it at the time, I never thought they'd be capable of something like this…"

His voice trailed off and he appeared to have fallen asleep.

The poor man, it would be months before he would be well enough to work again. What if he was right and someone did this deliberately to keep him from discovering the truth about her mother? Surely that couldn't be the case? Was her grandfather so devious that he would arrange to have a man killed to stop him exposing the crime he had committed against his own daughter?

Annie leant next to Dermot and whispered in his ear.

"I've made a decision; I'm going to check out Rosemont by myself."

His bloodshot eyes flew open and she could see the fear in them. He reached out to her and tried to sit up but the effort made him moan in pain. His voice was hoarse.

"You shouldn't risk it Annie. He tried to have me killed. What's to say he won't do the same to you?"

She left the hospital and took a taxi straight to the police station where Dermot's injuries had been reported. She was in luck. She arrived there just as the officer she was to ask for was getting ready to go off duty. Dermot had remembered that the name of the first policeman to arrive at the scene of his accident was Brian O'Reilly. Annie headed for the desk and asked for him by name. She told the desk sergeant what it was about and was asked to wait in a small room off the main reception area.

Officer O'Reilly arrived with Dermot's file. He was very Irish looking with coal black curly hair and blue eyes. Annie guessed he was about thirty. He quickly studied the woman before him, thrilled with his luck. It wasn't every day that he got to meet someone as stunningly attractive as her.

Annie introduced herself and he held her hand much longer than was necessary until, embarrassed, she finally pulled it away. She asked if they could talk about Dermot's accident. The police station was bustling with activity and the noise was deafening so Annie suggested a restaurant or pub? He said he would meet her across the street at Rosie's Café as soon as he changed his clothes. He was now technically *off duty*.

She crossed the street to the café, sat at a booth and ordered a coffee while she waited. He arrived quickly in casual clothes with Dermot's file still in his hand. He offered Annie a cigarette, which she refused, and asked if she'd mind if he smoked. She shook her head and he lit up, sucked in the smoke, felt his body relax and sat back, studying the woman in front of him with the file on the table between them.

"Now," he said, smiling. "What seems to be the trouble?"

She looked him straight in the eye.

"Do you believe that Dermot's hit-and-run was an accident or attempted murder?"

He looked surprised.

"What ever gave you the idea that it was anything more than an unfortunate car accident? I'd say it's a case of someone panicking after they hit him."

She studied him carefully.

"Dermot says that someone had been following him and was in the pub watching us the day he was injured. He said he gave you a full description of the man."

The officer looked uncomfortable.

"If you want to know what I think, I think he's being a wee bit paranoid. It's a normal reaction after something like this happens to you."

He opened the file and she saw the only thing on it was Dermot's name and address and a few perfunctory entries regarding the accident.

"But you haven't registered anything about the man Dermot says was following us."

He looked sheepish.

"Your friend tried to blame his accident on a well-known attorney with an exemplary background. You can understand my reluctance to contact a man such as Edward Ryan about this…err…misadventure."

As she listened to his reasoning about why he hadn't followed up on the information or made a note of the man who hit Dermot, she knew he had no intention of checking the man out. He was either afraid or…suddenly it hit her…she was talking to a man who was probably on her grandfather's payroll.

She stood up and made ready to leave. Feeling disappointed, he joined her.

"Would you like to go out to dinner with me sometime?"

She turned and faced him, very surprised.

"I'm afraid that's out of the question, I'm already in a relationship."

"Ah well," he sighed. "You can't blame a man for trying."

That night Annie had a difficult time getting to sleep and she went downstairs in the middle of the night for a glass of milk. She was surprised to find Mary there in her nightdress and robe, sitting at the table drinking a cup of tea.

"Tea will keep you awake, Mammy."

Mary looked up her.

"Do you realise that's the first time you've called me Mammy since you read that dreadful letter?"

Tears appeared in her eyes.

"I've missed my lovely daughter so much. I hate him for what he did to us both."

Annie was surprised at the emotion in her stepmother's voice.

Mary wiped her eyes with a tissue and put it in the pocket of her pink chenille robe.

"It was the way he kept us apart when you were a child that I hated most. He took you away from me, he never let us bond; he took you from me and kept you all to himself. He played us off against each other."

They sat quietly, not speaking, and when she had finished her tea she stood up and stretched.

"I'm all cried out; I'm off to bed."

As Annie said goodnight, she realised that she was as much to blame as her father. She had never really bothered to get to know Mary.

"Why don't we fly to Paris on Friday," she said. "I've already booked the tickets. I'd bought them originally for you and Daddy. I'd really love to show you the city, it's so beautiful."

Mary's face lit up with anticipation.

"I've always wanted to go there, it sounds wonderful. But what about your search for news of your mother?"

Just to see the delight on her stepmother's face was enough for Annie.

"This is more important. I'll continue looking when we get back next week, when Sean can join me. It will be a lot easier with him along."

"You two are becoming quite an item," Mary replied, smiling. "I'm so happy for both of you. He's a wonderful young man. I'm so glad you've found each other again."

Annie blushed and whispered: "So am I."

The next morning Annie received a telephone call from Terri in England. She sounded very upset and agitated.

"James has been paroled early. He's already out of prison. He broke into our flat when I was at work yesterday and tore the place apart. I think he did it out of spite. He found my address book; it was open at the page with your address and telephone number in Ireland. I'm really worried. I've already contacted the police here and they've checked his last known address. His clothes are gone and they've issued a notice for his arrest for breaking and entering. I'm scared. I think he could be heading for Ireland."

Annie listened 'til her friend had finished.

"Calm yourself, Terri. If he shows up here, it will mean he's broken his parole and he'll end up back in jail again. I don't think he'd be that foolish."

"I hope you're right," her roommate sighed.

Annie asked her how he managed to get into their flat. Terri sounded embarrassed.

"He told the doorman he was my husband and wanted to surprise me for my birthday—so the man let him in."

"What an idiot," Annie replied. "I hope you sorted him out."

"Yes, I was fuming and told him he could have been responsible for my death. It's just lucky I was away filming a commercial at the time. James must have got tired of waiting there for me to get back and left."

Annie wasn't listening anymore. She was busy thinking about James and wondering what he'd do next.

"I want you to have the locks changed. He might have copied our keys…and I want you to tell Christian what happened. Promise me you'll tell him everything, OK? Promise me?"

Terri promised, then calmed down and spoke about the business. It seemed that Terri was a natural. She had already turned a profit in their latest store but, after she hung up, Annie felt uneasy and worried about what would happen next. She got herself dressed to go out.

Mary had already left the house, eager to buy a new suitcase ready for their trip to Paris, so Annie decided she would pay Dermot another visit in hospital. She found him looking a little better and quizzed him again about the man who had been following them.

He described him as being about six feet tall, with blonde hair and a beard. Without realising it, he had described James, Terri's ex. It wasn't her grandfather who had put the poor man in the hospital. It had been James, getting his revenge.

But why had he targeted Dermot? After all, she was the one who had put him in prison. She explained this to Dermot and said she would report the possibility that James was responsible for the hit-and-run to the Irish police as soon as she left the hospital.

Again she took a taxi to the police station and asked for Officer O'Reilly. The desk sergeant buzzed him and Annie heard him whisper something about 'your girlfriend' into the telephone. O'Reilly came out with a bounce in his step.

She greeted him excitedly. "I have some news for you on the hit-and-run driver."

He ushered her into the small meeting room again and they sat facing each other.

"I know the hit-and-run driver," she said.

"He's here from London and he's my roommate's ex-husband; he just got out of prison for assault and battery. I was the one who helped put him there and he's come to Ireland with plans to hurt me."

The officer made notes as she spoke and, when he'd finished, looked up with a worried expression.

"But, if that's the case, why did he target Dermot."

She had been chewing this over herself and the only thing she had come up with was that he was targeting her family and thought that Dermot was one of them. That meant her brother; sister and stepmother could also be in danger.

Officer O'Reilly asked if she'd give a description of James to a police artist. She nodded and he phoned for the man to join them. In a matter of minutes the drawing was finished and his interpretation of James was very accurate. O'Reilly said he would have the likeness put on television and in the newspapers as quickly as possible. And he would also talk to his sergeant about having a policeman on watch outside her house until James was apprehended. He had already decided who that officer would be. He planned to ask his superior officer if he could take on that pleasant duty himself.

Annie left the police station feeling relieved. She was optimistic that the police would be able to catch James before he could do any more damage. He would be in for a shock when he saw his picture plastered all over the newspapers and on TV on Irish Crime Watch! Now she had to protect her family at all costs.

Her brother had gone on tour with Sean's band so he was safe enough, and she would include her sister Emily in their trip to Paris. They were leaving early in the morning on Air France and she would make sure they had a wonderful time in Paris. She realised she was probably worrying for nothing. By the time they returned from France, James could be in police custody.

There was only tonight to worry about.

After dinner she telephoned Sean and her brother before their show and told them of the Paris trip. They both thought it was a great idea. She omitted telling them about James.

CHAPTER 15

Later that evening, Mary and Annie were in the back room downstairs getting packed and Emily was upstairs in her bedroom. Emily had just finished packing and had her suitcase ready when the front door bell rang. She yelled that she would get it.

Mary smiled at Annie.

"It's her young man."

Emily raced downstairs. She had recently started dating Brendan Dunne, a nice enough young lad who had a thing for her. He'd told her he might come around that evening, before she left for France.

The second she threw the door open she knew she had made a terrible mistake. A police officer was pushed through the door and fell against her. She screamed when she saw the blood. His face and throat were covered in it. Standing directly behind him was a clean-shaven blonde-haired man, holding a large bloody hunting knife. He pushed the unwilling policeman ahead of him into the hallway and grabbed Emily by the throat. He held the knife against her chest as she let out a terrified cry for help.

Annie and her mother heard the scream. Mary wanted to rush to help her daughter, but Annie pulled her back and put a finger to her lips. Very quickly and quietly she picked up the telephone and dialled the police.

James was still struggling with the young squirming girl in his arms. Where was the woman he'd come for? He pushed Emily ahead of him into the living room, still holding firmly on to her.

There was no sign of the bitch that had ruined his life. She had to be here, he'd seen her go into the house earlier. It was time to use the young girl to flush her out.

"If your sister wants you to die, she's going about it the right way," he roared in a loud, threatening voice.

"I'm going to count to ten and, if she doesn't show herself, I guess I'll just have to start by slitting your throat."

Mary was about to cry when Annie placed her hand over her mother's mouth. They heard him begin his countdown and she made a decision. She couldn't take the chance that he wouldn't do what he said. She couldn't risk her sister's life. He had already gone too far with the attempted murder of Dermot. There was a long prison term facing him, and he had nothing to lose.

She knew James was a bully and a wife-beater but had never thought him capable of murder. She grabbed a container of Mace she always carried in her purse and hid it in the belt around her waist. Then she made her way cautiously into the living room.

James smiled when he saw her. Annie glared back at him scornfully.

"You don't want *her*, James, you've come for me. Am I right?"

She looked him straight in the eye, sounding calm but screaming inside. Her tone drove him crazy. The bitch thought she could bargain with him; he'd show her. After he killed her, he'd do the same to the rest of them.

"Let her join her mother in the other room."

He reluctantly released Emily and, as the young girl scurried out of the room, James tossed aside the knife he'd used on Officer O'Reilly, quickly replacing it with a small gun from his coat pocket. Now Annie and the unconscious O'Reilly were alone with him.

Still quaking inside, she spoke angrily.

"Were you the one who hit my friend with your car last week?"

James's face turned red with anger. He had come here to kill the bitch that had ruined his life and she had the nerve to question *him*.

"You mean your brother, the fat creep in the pub? Yeah, I fixed him good."

He was trying to keep his hand from shaking as he pointed the gun towards her. Annie was desperate to keep him talking. She knew if he pulled the trigger she would die instantly. She had to find a way to keep him talking until the police arrived. It was her only chance.

"He wasn't my brother, he was a journalist from *The Star*. You almost killed an innocent man."

She glanced over at the corner of the room where O'Reilly lay dying; his face and throat were covered in blood. He appeared unconscious. She pointed to him.

"What have you done to him? Did you shoot him?"

James looked at the young officer in disgust and shook his head.

Gloating, he replied: "Calls himself a policeman? He's a bloody idiot. He was supposed to be protecting you and I caught him smoking a cigarette on the pavement in front of your house. He didn't even recognise me. All I had to do was ask him for a light and, as he reached for his lighter, I stabbed him in the throat and dragged him inside."

Annie noticed that James had shaved off his beard. There was a sneer on his face as he studied the injured man.

Annie couldn't wait any longer; she decided it was time to strike. He was still smirking when she rushed at him, spraying his face and eyes with Mace. Then she made a dive for cover as he grabbed for his eyes, dropping the gun. It went flying across the room, landing a foot away from O'Reilly who had been feigning unconsciousness, patiently waiting his opportunity. He grabbed the gun in a flash and pointed it at James who reached for his knife on the floor and screamed that he was going to kill them all. O'Reilly fired just once, hitting the man full in the chest and he keeled over, dead.

Then all hell broke lose as various police officers rushed through the front door into the parlour.

Annie ran into the bathroom, grabbed a clean towel and raced back to where O'Reilly lay bleeding. He still had the gun when the police arrived and was passing out from loss of blood. She used the towel to apply pressure and stem the wound.

Her hand shook and she felt as if she would faint; but she continued the pressure—she had to try and save his life. None of this would have happened if it weren't for her. Two men had been badly injured because she hadn't believed that James could be dangerous.

Her mother and sister had rushed into the parlour at the sound of the commotion and they watched as she worked on the officer. Her stepmother looked pale and shaken and Annie suggested she sit down. She was praying out loud that the young officer would make it as the dead man's body was dragged from the front room.

Just when Annie felt she couldn't go on any longer, an ambulance screamed to a halt in front of their house. Two paramedics jumped out and rushed through the open front door carrying a stretcher and life support equipment.

Annie staggered to her feet and slumped into a chair. She was still holding the blood-soaked towel on her knee. She put her head into her hands and burst into tears. In a second Mary was next to her, petting her daughter gently.

"There...there...my darling girl. You were wonderful, you're such a brave girl, I'm so proud of you."

Hearing those words made Annie cry even harder. She was filled with love for her family, and so relieved that they were all safe.

"Oh, Mammy, I was so afraid he'd kill us, he had nothing to lose. Thank God my Mace worked, I was terrified it wouldn't work. I'd never used it before...You can still see my hands shaking...Thank God it worked!"

Sean called her that evening and Annie delayed telling him about their dreadful ordeal. She knew it would only worry him and he might pull out of his tour if he knew what had happened.

The local police station had sent a man to repair their front door.

CHAPTER 16

The three women took an early taxi to the Dublin Airport the next morning and boarded their Air France flight to Charles de Gaulle airport. They would be staying at the Ritz, one of the world's finest hotels. They were looking forward to trying the hotel's health club, swimming pool and squash courts.

The first thing Annie did on arrival was to arrange hair appointments, manicures and pedicures for the three of them. Later that afternoon she took them to the Pierre Cardin boutique on Rue du Faubourg Saint—Honoré and they then spent the rest of the afternoon shopping. Emily had been studying French in school and did her best to explain to the salesgirls what sort of clothes they were looking for and their sizes.

She was doing well with the language and the French saleswomen appreciated it and were very friendly and helpful to them.

The next stop was the Chanel boutique and, eventually, they left, loaded down with packages and wearing some of their new clothes. The shopping binge was expensive, but Annie enjoyed every minute of their spending spree.

By now they were hungry, so they dropped their packages off at the hotel and Annie took them to Maxims for dinner. It was her first time in the magnificent Le Grill room too. Mary looked around, taking in the wonderful décor and whispered excitedly: "I love Paris. Thank you so much for bringing us here."

As Annie studied her stepmother, she couldn't help noticing how much younger she was looking. Gone was the mousy grey hair. In its place was a stylish head of streaked pale blonde—and she was wearing make-up for the first time in years. Her new light blue tweed Chanel suit really complemented her elegant, almost-youthful, look.

Emily looked like a young Michelle Pfeiffer with *her* new haircut—and the pale pink Chanel suit she was now wearing. Annie was enjoying their company and felt very proud of them. She also noticed how much they were enjoying each other's company; they were acting more like friends, while Emily had dropped the moody teen pose and was acting very grown-up.

They ate a sumptuous dinner and sipped some premium wines. Annie felt that her relationship with Mary had improved tremendously over the past few weeks. She understood her stepmother much better now and felt Mary was an amazing woman. How many women would have done what she did; take her husband's lovechild into her home and raise her as her own? It took a special kind of person to forgive a man his indiscretions and then take on his unwanted illegitimate child.

That night they dressed up in their new gowns. They were going to the magnificent Paris Opera House. *Carmen* was playing that particular night. Annie explained that the theatre in *The Phantom of the Opera* was actually based on the Paris Opera House.

Annie wore a long, pink satin dress and Emily looked like a tiny French model with her hair up, wearing the lovely plum coloured lace mini dress; and when Mary finally made her shy entrance into the room, she was wearing a stunning black silk crepe dress, adorned with jet beads and matching earrings and bracelet.

The two girls gave low whistles and exclaimed together: "Wow…Mammy, you're a knockout!" Emily couldn't help wishing that her father were there to see how lovely her mother looked.

The opera and the whole evening was a great success and their relationship continued to flourish.

The following morning, Annie and Emily played tennis at the hotel courts. Mary was sitting quietly at a table in the shade watching them when the waiter brought her a glass of champagne. She told him that she hadn't ordered champagne, and he pointed to the veranda where a distinguished looking older gentleman raised his glass to her. She blushed, feeling flattered. It had been years since a man had paid her any attention. She raised her glass back to him with a demure smile on her lips. He came over and joined her. He was about her age, tall with silver hair and a moustache. He introduced himself as Armand. He was French and, speaking with a sexy accent the way only Frenchmen do, they spent the next two hours together sipping Champagne and chatting. Later, when the girls left the court and headed for the showers to change, he got up to leave.

But, before he left, he asked Mary if she would consider going out with him? He would love to show her around Paris, his beautiful city, the following day. Mary studied the handsome man standing next to her and, feeling slightly tipsy and very flattered by his attention, she agreed.

The next day Annie helped her get ready for her date with Armand. She wore an off-white wool crepe skirt with a pink and cream top, topped off with a soft leather jacket in cream. Annie thought her stepmother looked wonderful. She had checked out the man that Mary was going on the date with (after James she didn't want to take any chances). She didn't have to worry; the man was a widower, recently retired. He had been a pilot with Air France.

Mary was like a young girl on her first date, so filled with excitement, and Annie was happy that she was seeing such a nice man.

All three of them had benefited enormously from the trip and, two days later, they left Paris to fly home to Dublin. Armand saw Mary off at the airport. They had spent two wonderful days together and he promised to visit her when he was in Dublin on business, in a month's time.

They were sad leaving Paris behind, but happy that their short holiday had brought them all closer together.

Sean returned from his tour two days later and headed straight for Annie's house. He had already heard from her brother what happened with James and recognized how close he had come to losing her. The thought of that, so soon after they had found each other again, terrified him.

He had a month off before his next German tour and decided to spend as much time as possible with her. With the time available he knew they ought to be able to find out a good deal of information about her mother. Annie would be safe as long as she was with him.

She was delighted to have him back, but there was one more thing she had to take care of before they left for Cork. She needed to visit Dermot in hospital, to let him know it was James, not her grandfather, who had run him over. Sean said he wanted to go with her.

They arrived at the Mater Hospital and went directly to Ward 6, but were surprised to see a new patient in Dermot's bed. Annie asked one of the nurses where Dermot was. Had they moved him to another floor? The nurse said she was new; she had just started working there but told them the only person she'd seen in that bed was her current patient, Johnny O'Toole. She didn't know anything about a Dermot Moore.

Annie felt very uneasy. Surely he hadn't passed away? He was young and strong but, then again, he had been very badly injured. Worried about what had become of him, they went to the *In-Patient Department* office and were told a relative had checked Dermot out. Annie demanded to speak with the doctor who had signed his release form and, as luck would have it, he was still making his rounds.

He arrived a few minutes later and gave them the same story. A relative had indeed signed Dermot out, even though the doctor had said his patient was not really well enough to be moved. The man wouldn't listen, insisting it was what Dermot wanted. He said he had already hired a full-time nurse for his cousin and she would take care of him at home. The patient seemed to go along with what had been said, although he appeared to be 'a bit out of it' at the time.

Alarm bells rang in Annie's head as she listened to the doctor. He had to get back to his rounds and left them in the matron's hands.

"What was the man's name?" Annie asked, sensing that the matron was anxious to get rid of them.

Getting no obvious reply, she repeated her question.

"What was the man's name who checked Dermot out?"

She checked the register nervously herself, but the only signature she could find was Dermot's uneven scrawl.

"So this imaginary relative never actually signed the register."

Annie looked at the woman in disgust.

"So how do you know the so-called relative was for real?"

The matron replied smugly.

"It's not our practice to check out people's relatives when the patient tells us it's OK by them."

Annie was disgusted with her attitude and turned to Sean.

"Let's go, we're wasting our time here."

She then looked directly at the woman and spoke.

"You're a disgrace to the medical profession. You had better pray that Dermot is OK or you and the hospital are in serious trouble. You have allowed a seriously ill patient to leave this hospital, and you admit *he was out of it*. And you have no record or signature of the person he left with. Surely you must be aware that someone tried to kill him?"

She turned her back on the woman and headed straight for the exit. She was still fuming and, when Sean suggested it might have been a relative, her eyes sparked with anger.

"Don't tell me you agree with these idiots! How could they release a man in Dermot's condition from the hospital? You didn't see how ill he was Sean, I did! When I went to see him, he told me that someone was trying to kill him, and then a week later he's missing."

Annie didn't know where the journalist lived. She decided to visit the newspaper offices and speak to the editor of the paper. Surely he would have his address.

At the reception desk, Annie said she wanted to speak to the editor regarding Dermot Moore, and minutes later they were escorted into his office. Michael O'Brien seemed nervous as he directed them to the two chairs in front of his desk.

"Please take a seat. What's Dermot done now?" he asked timidly.

Annie looked surprised.

"I don't know what you mean. Dermot's a friend of mine. Is it usual to ask a question like that about an employee?"

The editor looked surprised.

"But he doesn't work here any more. I fired him weeks ago."

Now it was Annie's turn to look surprised.

"But he said he worked for *The Star* when we met. He had some information about my mother, Jacqueline Ryan."

Michael O'Brien looked stunned. So the child did exist, this was Jacqueline's daughter. Maybe Dermot had been right after all.

He felt remorseful. Why had he let Edward Ryan bully him into firing the man? He had never really given the journalist a chance. He felt angry with himself for letting Ryan control him.

Why did he listen to Ryan instead of being open to what Dermot had to say?

He knew the young man was a good reporter who wouldn't go off half-cocked; he was sure he would have researched Ryan, before going for an interview. He felt ashamed of himself; he was supposed to be a newspaperman and, instead, he was a sorry excuse for a man.

As he studied the attractive young couple sitting in front of him, he decided to come clean and tell them the whole story, how Edward Ryan had bullied and threatened him into firing Dermot.

When Annie told him about Dermot's terrible accident and his disappearance from the hospital, he promised he'd put some of his research people on it right away. They generally knew what was going on out in the streets.

Annie left her address and telephone number with O'Brien and begged him to get in touch if he heard anything. She was given Dermot's telephone number, his home address and his mother's address.

CHAPTER 17

Once again Edward and Elizabeth Ryan found themselves discussing the young reporter.

"Why on earth did you arrange for Frank Hunt, of all people, to move him out of the hospital?" Elizabeth asked angrily.

"Have you gone completely mad, finally taken leave of your senses? Don't you know what that man's like? He's a gossip! What do you think he's doing right now? Our business will be all over Dublin by tomorrow morning."

Edward's face was flushed as he faced his wife and he tried desperately to control the anger he felt towards her. The bloody woman questioned everything he did lately.

He leaner closer to her,

"So what did I do that was so wrong?" he asked petulantly.

"I put the journalist into an expensive nursing home, where he'll get the best care and treatment, and they'll also keep him out of my hair. I suppose you would have been happier if I'd killed him."

"Don't lie to me, Edward, you didn't do it to help him. You had the man locked up in a place where they'll keep him drugged and out of it so he'll be no threat to you."

Elizabeth studied her husband's face and felt nothing but loathing. She hadn't felt any love for him in a long time and now he had become a detriment to her future. If he was allowed to continue on his merry way they might both end up in jail. It was time she took control; then, after everything was sorted, she would get out.

After all, she was the one with the money. She had the most to lose. She had fooled herself into thinking that she still loved this pig-headed man.

"You want to know what I would have done. I'd have left him where he was, in hospital. He was so out of it; he wouldn't have been any threat to you for months. But no, you had to play the big man and take things into your own hands. You're a fool, Edward!"

She couldn't hide her true feelings any longer. She felt nothing but disgust for him. As she stood staring defiantly at him, he was stunned by the hatred he saw in her face.

She turned and left the room, slamming the door behind her.

CHAPTER 18

Annie and Sean arrived at Dermot's flat early the following morning. They rang the bell and, when there was no answer, they decided to try the janitor's office. His bell wasn't working either, so Sean banged loudly on the door until a large bull of a man with the look of an ex-police officer eventually opened the door to them. He was still dressed in his nightclothes and stared angrily at Sean.

"What the hell do you want, waking a man from his sleep in the middle of the night?"

Annie moved in front of Sean and the man softened when he'd got a good look at her.

"Sorry miss, I didn't see you there."

He was still grumpy. She smiled sweetly.

"I was looking for Dermot in Flat 3 but he doesn't answer his door."

"So what do you want me to do about it?"

Annie turned on her charm and replied: "We're both very worried about him. I don't know if you know that he was seriously injured in a car accident and shouldn't be left alone."

The man was surprised and this seemed to change his mind about getting involved.

"Wait a minute, I'll get dressed. I'll get the keys to his flat and let you in."

A couple of minutes later he was back, dressed in jeans and a sweater. He beckoned them and they followed him. When he opened Dermot's door, he let out a gasp.

"What the hell…"

The flat had been vandalized and whoever did it must have been pretty desperate to find whatever it was they were looking for. The sofa and chairs were turned upside down and the fabric ripped apart. Even the carpet had been pulled up. But there was definitely no sign of Dermot having been there recently.

Sean and Annie left the man to sort out the flat. They were now even more worried about him. What had happened? Was he dead or alive?

During the short drive home they discussed what to do next. Should they go to the police? Annie shook her head.

"Poor Dermot. What do you think happened to him? Do you think he's dead?"

Sean glanced at her thoughtfully and shook his head.

"I think he's still very much alive and, when we find your mother, we'll find Dermot. I hate to say it but I believe this time your grandfather *is* involved."

"But surely he wouldn't be *that* stupid. Do you think we should go and talk to him?"

Sean shook his head.

"No, I don't think we should let him know we're on to him. I do think we should take a good look at the nursing home, the one Dermot told you about. Maybe we can talk Mary into helping us."

Annie looked surprised.

"How can she help us?"

Sean just smiled.

"Your stepmother has a unique talent that most people don't even know about."

Annie was really curious now and, when they finally arrived at the house in Phibsboro, Sean stopped the car and turned towards her with a smile.

"I have a plan that might just work!"

CHAPTER 19

Rosemont Nursing Home was built in 1894, an elegant Victorian structure standing in twenty-five acres of lush green land on the outskirts of Cork. A tree-lined driveway wound its way towards the main building.

When Sean, Mary and Annie arrived, the front of the place was alive with white-clad nurses, out with their patients enjoying the early morning sunshine. Nurses and nurse's aids were moving a steady stream of wheelchair-bound individuals around the garden and in and out of the main building.

Annie looked worried as she studied Mary.

"Are you sure you can carry it off?"

Mary put her arm around her stepdaughter.

"Sure I can, darling. I've had lots of acting experience. I got into it the year you left for London and I've never looked back. I love playing a different character. I was in *Juno and the Peacock* just last year. Anyway, it's not hard to play an old lady when that's what you are."

Annie studied her and saw that she was right. Mary had made herself look years older than her actual age. They might well get away with it. She was dressed in a dowdy long grey skirt and old cardigan and wore a grey wig that resembled a helmet. Her body language was old and decrepit and she walked bent forward, as though she didn't have the energy to stand up straight anymore. The change in her stepmother's appearance was startling. She did look like a woman desperately needing help.

So Sean's plan was put into action. Annie had already met Miss Pritchard, the manager of Rosemont. She found her a rather dour looking string bean of a woman who wore the look of someone who hated the whole world.

Annie had explained that her mother had become very forgetful of late and required full-time care. She was allergic to most things but did not require medicine of any sort (she didn't want the woman feeding Mary pills to keep her quiet). Annie just needed her mother out of the house to give the other members of the family a rest. When she expressed her willingness to pay whatever it took to see that her mother received the best care available, the woman's eyes lit up and she smiled for the first time.

Miss Pritchard was used to families trying to cut costs on their relative's care and was thrilled with her new client. She was only too happy to welcome Mary and take her off their hands. She would make sure that the woman was placed in one of their nicer rooms. And if she could slip her a little medication so she didn't want to leave, so much the better.

Sean's plan was simple. As soon as Mary was settled in, she was to make a point of getting to know some of the nurses and other residents. She would find out what she could as regards Dermot, and about Annie's mother Jacqueline. Sean was convinced that they were probably both at the place.

After the young couple left Rosemont, and Mary was settled in her room, she lay on her bed thinking. It was ironic that she should be the one who was asked to find the woman who had ruined her life and her marriage. Her mind raced back over the years to her first years as a young bride. Why had it been so important to her that she get pregnant right away? She shook her head. It wasn't Jacqueline who had ruined her marriage, she had done it all by herself.

She pushed John away when she didn't conceive. It was her desperate need for a baby that had ruined their marriage.

Perhaps it was her Catholic upbringing and the doctrine that had been drummed into her head by her mother. The woman had been a religious zealot, believing that sex within a marriage was strictly for procreation and should not be used for any other reason. Why had she listened to her?

They were married two and a half years when he told her he couldn't take it any longer. Their lovemaking was too clinical for him. She was only willing to make love when she was sure she was ovulating and he was sick of the idea that each time they made love it was to make a baby. He wanted to make love to her for other reasons than just to procreate.

John didn't feel like a man anymore. His confidence was at an all-time low, so he had packed his bags and moved out. He found a flat in Galway and set up The Tudor Tennis Club with his young friend Tim O'Shea. The club became successful and he began to feel young again.

He was excited and happy that he was making a success of a business he loved. There was even talk of them getting back together again.

Mary visited him in Galway and they made love, and when it was over and they were in each other's arms, she asked him if he would come back to her. He studied her carefully before answering.

"Can you forget about the baby for the time being?"

She hesitated, knowing that if she told him the truth it would be the end of their life together, but she couldn't lie to him.

"I still want a baby."

It was still the most important thing in her life.

Two weeks later he met Jacqueline and they fell in love. He sounded like a schoolboy when he gave his wife the news. It hurt her deeply, seeing his eyes filled with excitement and love when he spoke about another woman. He told Mary that he was in love for the first time in his life. His words hurt her so deeply that she wanted to die.

Then the pain she felt turned to jealousy and filled her heart with hate; but, somehow, she managed to hide her feelings in front of him.

How could he fall in love with a sixteen-year-old girl? She tried to warn him that he was courting danger messing about with someone underage. Then he had got the girl pregnant. And her hatred for the girl who had stolen her husband and was having the child that should have been hers grew. Why hadn't she been the one he made pregnant?

When he told her that, because he was going to be a father, they intended moving to England, she wanted to kill both of them. Then he had the nerve to ask her for help; he wanted her to go over to England and get a quick divorce, so he could marry her rival. He would pay for her return fare. She wanted to bash his face in…how could be so thoughtless?

She lied, saying she would help them and there were no hard feelings. But, when he left, she broke everything in the house she could get her hands on. She hated him for not seeing what he had done to her. She wanted to punish both of them. She had dressed quickly and that very day she went to see Jacqueline's parents and told them everything.

Two days later John arrived at her house in a terrible state. He told her that Jacqueline had run off with his tennis partner Tim, and now he wasn't even sure if the baby was his. When he calmed down, she got the whole story. He had arranged for Tim to meet Jacqueline, reasoning that Tim was closer to Jacqueline's age and, if her father saw them together, he wouldn't think anything bad. John would meet the two of them later that day at a restaurant in Galway. The only problem was neither of them had shown up as planned. He sat in the restaurant where they were supposed to meet for hours, praying there was nothing wrong.

A couple of days later, Tim's body washed up on shore but there was no sign of Jacqueline. After Tim's death, John had turned to Mary and they got back together again. He never knew that she was the one who had tipped off Jacqueline's parents.

Mary had never felt right about what she did. Through her jealousy she had probably caused Tim's death and Jacqueline's incarceration. Perhaps that was why she had to be the one to try to find the woman now. She may have been the reason the girl had been put away, spending twenty-five years in this awful place. Jacqueline had missed out on so many things because of her, including raising her own daughter.

As Annie got older, she looked more and more like the photographs that John had shown her of Jacqueline. The girl had been a constant reminder of the guilt Mary felt about what she had done. What would happen when Annie found out her dirty little secret? Their relationship was so much better now. What if Jacqueline remembered seeing Mary with her parents that day? She shivered at the thought. She had wasted so many years feeling guilty. It was all John's fault.

What should she do? If she found Jacqueline, her secret would be out. But then again, this was maybe her one and only chance to make amends to John and Jacqueline, some kind of redemption.

Then she thought, to hell with both of them. What about her? John had ruined her life and Jacqueline had been a big part of it. Why should she feel the need to find her? She would be better off left where she was...for all their sakes. If the woman had been in this hellhole for twenty-five years she was probably so institutionalised she simply wouldn't be able to handle life on the outside. She could say she had no luck, why not leave her here.

CHAPTER 20

Elizabeth Ryan was with her accountant James Black, a tall handsome man in his early forties. Theirs was a great deal more than just a business relationship. James had fallen hard for Elizabeth's money and her good looks. He wasn't so keen on her formidable personality. He was a gambler and enjoyed spending money as quickly as he could make it, so her financial net worth certainly was the icing on the cake for him.

When they first began their affair she had been starved for sex and couldn't get enough of him. It had been years since Edward had touched her or shown any sexual interest in her. James and Elizabeth usually met at his office or at his apartment on Merrion Square. He had asked her to move in with him a number of times and leave her husband, but so far she had always refused. Now, thankfully, it appeared that she might have had a change of heart.

Elizabeth studied him, carefully noting the handsome face with the slightly weak chin. He was a good-looking man and a good lover who had served her well.

"I've decided to leave him, James. If I do leave, where will that put me financially?"

He moved from behind his desk and took her in his arms.

"In a very good place, my pet. You own sixty per cent of his law firm, and there's about five million in bearer bonds in your name. I'd say, with your stocks, bonds and equity in real estate, you're looking at around thirty million Euros. If you wanted to, you could force Edward out of the company. You own the controlling shares."

Elizabeth smiled slyly.

"We could have a lot of fun with that kind of money. But what about the tax ramifications if I take over the business?"

James answered quickly, filled with anticipation. He was going to be rich after all. He'd put a little bet on the gee-gees as soon as she left; he could afford it now. He smiled, his mind racing to say the right thing.

"That's where I come in, my dear," he said, unbuttoning her blouse. I'll take good care of you and the taxman. I don't want you worrying your pretty little head about anything?"

CHAPTER 21

Edward Ryan was enjoying his breakfast and was reading the morning newspaper when Elizabeth entered the room. He looked up, surprised to see her up and about at seven in the morning. It was so unlike her; she was a night person and normally didn't stir until after ten. What *was* she up to now?

"Where are you going at this ungodly hour?" he asked suspiciously. She gave him a withering look.

"It's really none of your business, Edward," she replied haughtily, leaving the room and slamming the door behind her.

He heard the front door slam and the engine of her car as she left the driveway. Minutes later there was the sound of a second car drawing up to the house. That would be Joe's car.

Joe Duggan was the detective he'd hired to keep an eye on Elizabeth. He had used the same man on numerous other occasions in the past and, although he was expensive, Edward knew he could count on him. If there were something going on, he would be the first to know about it.

If Elizabeth wasn't around for a few hours he would go and see Kathy; he missed her. She was like his mother—she didn't ask anything of him, just his love. Why hadn't he fallen for her originally instead of going after Elizabeth? He guessed it was because she was the forbidden fruit, the girl from the other side of the tracks. And when he found out that her father hated him and didn't want him anywhere near his daughter, it made him want her even more.

If only he'd known then what Elizabeth was really like, that she didn't have a heart and wasn't capable of showing real love or affection to her husband or children. The only thing she loved was money and the business. What a legacy he had left his children, no wonder their twin sons had moved to England to live. If he'd known what she was like he would have left as well.

CHAPTER 22

After her terrifying experience with Terri's ex-husband, Annie didn't want to spend time alone at the house in Dublin. She just couldn't bring herself to stay there; the house was filled with too many terrifying and unhappy memories.

She planned on buying her stepmother a new house when this business was over. It was the least she could do. Mary had already spent a week at Rosemont and Emily was away at school.

Annie was spending most of her time with Sean, at his house in Killiney.

His decor was ultra-modern and the house had fantastic views of the spectacular Irish coastline and the ever-changing sea. Killiney is a coastal town about twelve miles south of Dublin. And where else would a successful musician live?

They were so at ease with each other. Knowing she was there made Sean feel complete for the first time in his life. He was thinking seriously of asking her to marry him as soon as things settled down. They were deeply in love and so right for each other both mentally and physically.

Sexually he just couldn't get enough of her and she appeared to feel the same way about him. Life was good. If only they could find her mother, if, in fact, she was still alive.

It was eleven, on Monday morning. Mary was relaxing on the large wraparound porch when she noticed the Mercedes convertible. The car stopped in front of the main building and a good-looking woman got out. Mary couldn't help noticing the woman as she left the car. She was the most put-together senior citizen, she had seen in a long time. She must have been a stunner when she was younger. She put on her glasses to study the woman in more depth. There was something familiar about her. Where had she seen her before?

She had a hard time concentrating. She had felt so tired lately and couldn't think clearly. It was probably the surroundings and the lack of company.

Suddenly it came to her; the woman was Elizabeth Ryan. She was the woman Mary had met twenty-five years earlier regarding the relationship between her husband and the woman's daughter.

Now what could Jacqueline's mother be doing here? She looked a good deal older, but Mary was sure it was the same person. She was having a long conversation with Miss Pritchard. Mary tried to make out what they were talking about, but she was too far away to hear. Then the two women went inside.

Curious, she decided to follow them at a discreet distance.

She noticed that Miss Pritchard took Elizabeth Ryan down a separate passageway, away from the main nursing home. Mary had never been in this part of the building before and she figured that it was probably used for special patients.

The two women stopped at a door with a small glass panel. Miss Pritchard unlocked it and they both went inside. Mary heard footsteps and froze. She saw another door to the right of her. There was a key in the lock. She turned the key and slipped inside.

"Who are you?"

The slurred words came from a man lying in a hospital bed in the room. He looked like he'd been in a serious accident. Mary studied his chart. The name said Dermot Moore. She had inadvertently stumbled upon the reporter who had vanished from the Mater Hospital. She was so excited she forgot to be afraid anymore.

"I'm Mary, Annie's step-mother," she blurted out. "I'm here to help you but you mustn't let on that you've seen me." He nodded and Mary looked relieved; he understood why she was in his room.

"Annie and Sean are visiting me later today, I'll tell them where you are. Now I've got to go, before any of the staff find me here."

Opening the door and quickly glancing from side to side to check that the corridor was clear she left his room, locking the door again behind her. Then she headed towards the room she had seen Miss Pritchard and Elizabeth Ryan enter. She had to know if Jacqueline was in that room.

She edged along the dark passageway as quietly as she could and peered through a round glass panel in the door. Apparently, Miss Pritchard and Mrs Ryan had left, while she was in Dermot's room.

Mary could see that the room held a small table, two chairs and a television set; and, yes, there was a woman lying on a bed facing the door. As far as she could remember, the bed-ridden woman did bear a slight resemblance to Jacqueline, but years of drugs, poor food and lack of exercise had bloated her face and body. The years had not been kind to her. Mary noticed she was cuddling a doll the way a mother holds a new baby.

She would have loved to have gone into the room to speak to her but the guilt she felt for the pain and suffering she'd caused the poor woman wouldn't allow her to go inside. Tears began to roll down her face as she watched the woman kiss that old doll.

Mary made her way back to the main part of the hospital without incident. Mrs Ryan was still there, standing next to her car with Miss Pritchard. They were in deep conversation and, as Mary watched, the two women shook hands and Mrs. Ryan got into her Mercedes and drove off.

She was only just out of sight when an ambulance raced up the driveway and skidded to a halt in front of the hospital. Two orderlies got out, removed a stretcher from the back of the ambulance and raced into the hospital. Mary moved closer to see what was happening. Moments later they returned with Dermot on the stretcher. His head was bandaged but she could still see his eyes and when they met hers there was a look of sheer panic in them.

Where the hell were Annie and Sean? Why weren't they here? If they had been here they could have stopped them taking him away. Mary knew she could do nothing to help him without giving herself away and the ambulance left as quickly as it had arrived with its secret cargo.

Miss Pritchard was now standing by the door a few feet away and Mary moved slowly towards the woman. She was determined to find out what was going on.

"Where are they taking the poor soul, Miss Pritchard?" she asked, in the old lady voice she had used since she'd arrived at the home.

"Was the lovely lady in the fancy car his mother? The poor woman, she must be sick with worry."

Miss Pritchard studied the elderly woman facing her. Had the old bitch seen something? Could she cause them trouble? Ah, she was just being silly; the woman was a doddering old fool. And she kept her drugged up to the eyeballs. Who would believe anything she said? She gave Mary a contemptuous look.

"The ambulance has taken the gentleman to a medical hospital for treatment," she replied bluntly, before being called away inside by one of the nurses.

Annie and Sean arrived some time later and Mary told them what she had seen. She'd memorized the name on the side of the ambulance and Sean made a quick call on his mobile phone. He was told that Dermot had been taken to the intensive care ward at St. Vincent's Hospital.

Mary made a decision. She had to tell them about Jacqueline. Regardless of what happened in the past, the woman had suffered enough. She explained what she had seen. She couldn't be absolutely sure, but the woman could well be Jacqueline.

Annie wanted desperately to go straight to see her, but Sean said it was too risky. He felt the best way to handle things would be to first get to Dermot. When the police were told that he had been held at

Rosemont against his will, they would be obliged to get a search warrant to check the place out.

Sean thought his solicitor could probably arrange for Jacqueline to be released into her daughter's hands. He didn't want Annie stumbling into her mother's room and finding a woman who no longer functioned properly. From what Mary had said, Jacqueline appeared to have reverted back to her childhood and would need a lot of psychiatric help.

Sean asked Mary if she'd be willing to stay at Rosemont a little longer to keep an eye on Miss Pritchard. He was worried that the woman might get wind that something was up before they could get to the police and she'd move Jacqueline somewhere else.

Mary nodded. She was so tired lately, it seemed that all she wanted to do was sleep.

He gave Mary his mobile phone so she could keep in touch with him and she said she was content to play detective a bit longer. In a way she found it exciting.

CHAPTER 23

Annie and Sean drove from Cork to Dublin without stopping and their arrival at St. Vincent's Hospital coincided with visiting hours. Annie told the receptionist she was Dermot's sister and that Miss Pritchard at Rosemont had contacted her to say that her brother had been moved to St. Vincent's.

The woman checked her records. She looked worried and Annie thought she had guessed she wasn't related.

"Oh, dear," she said. "What a shame. It looks like your brother has had a very rough time of it. Never mind dear, we'll take good care of him here. He's in Room 234, that's on the second floor, down the corridor, third door on the left."

Relieved, Annie and Sean thanked her and headed for the stairs. Room 234 was a private room and Dermot was the only patient. A nurse was seated across the room from him. Annie guessed that her grandmother had hired her. Maybe she was worried about him. He did look dreadful, but at least he was sitting up in bed now.

His eyes were still bruised, but they lit up when he saw her. Before he could say anything, Annie turned to the nurse.

"I hope my brother hasn't given you any trouble."

The nurse was a motherly looking woman. She seemed relieved when Annie spoke to her. She had been feeling sorry for the poor man.

"Not at all, he just got here. Would you like me to leave you alone for a few minutes?"

Annie nodded and the nurse smiled and left the room. They moved closer to Dermot's bedside.

"You were right about Jacqueline," Annie whispered.

Dermot's voice was hoarse, but he responded excitedly.

"You mean you've found her?"

Annie brought him up-to-date on what had happened over the past week, the saga with James and how he died. She also told him that Mary had volunteered to enter Rosemont and was the person who found him—as well as finding Jacqueline.

"But how did I end up at Rosemont?" he asked.

"The last place I remember being was at the Mater Hospital."

Sean explained that he thought Edward Ryan had had one of his henchmen take the reporter to Rosemont by ambulance. He wanted Dermot watched to prevent him getting too close to the truth.

Obviously Elizabeth didn't agree with her husband. She was the one who had decided to move Dermot to St. Vincent's where he could get proper medical care.

The weird thing was that Edward Ryan had placed Dermot in Rosemont. And the reporter was right across the hall from Jacqueline. It was almost as if he wanted her to be found or maybe some perverse part of her grandfather's mind felt he could outsmart the reporter. It was like playing Russian roulette, just the sort of game her grandfather would enjoy playing.

Annie hated thinking what her unfortunate mother had suffered at his hands. Her mother was only forty-one, still a young woman. If it were at all possible, she would help her regain her life and her sanity.

Elizabeth had left Rosemont in a state of nervous exhaustion. She couldn't bring herself to head straight home and so kept driving. Her mind was filled with the memory of the way Jacqueline had looked in that drab, miserable room. *What had they done to her once, beautiful daughter?* Tears filled her eyes. She drove on automatically, not even noticing the road works and the numerous delays.

She bypassed the centre of Dublin and drove around the outskirts, heading for Howth, the seaside town where she had lived as a young child. Her family had moved upmarket when she was seven, but she always remembered the quiet beauty of the place.

After driving to the far end of the pier, she parked the Mercedes and turned off the engine. She couldn't get the picture of her daughter out of her mind. *That damned hospital had turned the girl into a pale washed-out old woman. Her large eyes were almost swollen shut; she was incoherent and drooled when she spoke.* For the first time in her life Elizabeth felt tremendous guilt over what had happened to her Jacqueline.

She should never have let Edward get away with it. He was the one responsible for what had happened to their daughter. Why hadn't she gone to the police? In her heart she knew it was because she couldn't bare the publicity that would follow. Everyone believed Edward was a saint who could do no wrong.

He had some powerful friends and, if the truth were told, she had been glad to get Jacqueline out of the way. The girl had brought shame on the family, getting herself pregnant. But she never imagined he would place her in such a filthy hole. Her mistake was in letting Edward handle things.

Elizabeth knew that she had never been a maternal woman, but he could have at least asked her advice before committing their daughter. She felt real hatred towards him at that moment. There was no turning back now, though, as she had moved Dermot Moore out of Rosemont.

She had been afraid that, if he was left at Rosemont, he wouldn't make it and she didn't want to be held responsible for the man's death. Her husband would be livid when he found out. She knew how spiteful he could be when he was thwarted.

She stifled a sob. It wasn't her fault that she wasn't maternal. In her own way she loved her children but she was never really close to any of them.

Her housekeeper, Bridget, was the one who raised Jacqueline and the twin boys, Edward Junior and David. And, as soon as they were old enough, Elizabeth had sent the boys away to the best boarding school money could buy. Her busy social life and the help she gave Edward building up his law practice just hadn't allowed time for raising children.

But Jacqueline had been different; she had always been a stubborn child, refusing to leave home like her brothers. She had insisted on attending a private school in their neighbourhood until it was time to go to college. Why hadn't she held firm and sent the girl away to school? If she had, all of this could have been avoided. She was still unclear in her mind how Jacqueline had suffered the nervous breakdown. She had only Edward's word about how it happened.

Deep down she knew she had been a coward and hadn't wanted to question him, in case the girl's breakdown had been caused by something dreadful that might reflect on her good name and their business.

It was bad enough that Jacqueline had got herself involved with a married man and gotten pregnant. The girl had been underage and Edward had threatened her lover with the police and jail for having carnal knowledge of a minor.

Jacqueline must have loved the man a lot because she agreed to go into a home for unwed mothers until the baby was born. She would have done anything, so long as they left her lover alone.

After the baby was born, her parents had bent over backwards for her. They even allowed her to keep her child as long as she stayed away from the father. If she didn't follow their rules, the child would be put up for adoption and her lover would be charged and receive a stiff prison sentence. Jacqueline had wept for her lover, but eventually agreed it was for the best.

And they had been as good as their word. They let her keep the child for two whole years until that dreadful day when everything went wrong.

Elizabeth delved deeply into her mind, trying to remember exactly what Edward told her about that day. He said he had followed Jacqueline to Galway, where she met a young man and they took the ferry over to Inish Mann. Edward said he found a local fisherman and paid him to take him over to the island so he could follow the young couple. When he got there, he headed for the place where he thought Jacqueline might be. It was a place he had taken the children when they were young. Elizabeth remembered those details clearly.

He said that he had heard Jacqueline scream and rushed to investigate. The young man was on top of her and it looked like he was trying to rape her. Edward pulled him off and a fight started. He said they were near the edge of the cliff and, during the fight, the young man lost his footing and slipped into the sea below.

Then he said he turned to his daughter. She was in a terrible state. She wouldn't stop crying and he realised she had probably suffered a nervous breakdown from the things she had just witnessed.

He never reported the death of the young man to the police. People drown everyday and a tasteless scene might have hurt his social standing in the community.

They placed Jacqueline in Rosemont to recuperate and later put her baby up for adoption. In a way, Elizabeth had felt a little better about it when she learned that the man who adopted the baby was the child's father. Let him take care of his responsibility; she had no time in her busy life to take care of another child.

The sad part about all this was that Jacqueline had never gotten over the loss of her baby. She didn't seem to comprehend that the child would now be a grown woman. She imagined that the old doll Miss Pritchard had given her was her little daughter Annie. It is really sad, the tricks the mind can play.

So Elizabeth supposed that her daughter would spend the rest of her life at Rosemont. She had admittedly been shocked to find how much her granddaughter resembled Jacqueline and, if she were anything like her mother, she'd be stubborn and wouldn't give up easy. They could expect trouble from that quarter.

If the whole sordid tale came out, she would be the laughing stock of the community. People that she didn't know, people she would never have dreamt of associating with, would be judging her.

It was all Edward's fault. He had ruined both of their lives. The hatred she felt towards him made her hands shake. She had to get free of him as soon as possible.

CHAPTER 24

Annie and Sean talked it over and decided it would be best if Annie met with the police and told them about her mother. Sean would bring his solicitor up-to-date. So they went their separate ways, Sean to get legal advice and Annie to her meeting with the police. She had already contacted them and set up an appointment to see the officer-in-charge.

When she arrived at the police station she was surprised and flattered by the reception she received. As she entered the door, there was a rousing round of applause and catcalls from men at the inquiries desk. They must have been expecting her.

Annie had saved the life of O'Reilly, one of their colleagues, and this was their way of showing their appreciation and gratitude. And she was not hard on the eye. She was wearing a short, pale yellow summer dress with sexy high-heel sandals that showed off her long, beautiful legs. She was taller than most of the officers there and, as a child, that would have bothered her terribly. Then one day she discovered that short men love tall women and had never worried about her height again.

Officer O'Reilly came in and took her hand. His face still showed the bruises from his encounter with James and his neck was still bandaged. As he steered her ahead of him into the conference room, he took pleasure inhaling the soft sweet fragrance of her perfume as she walked in front of him. He had to admit he was hooked. If only she wasn't committed to someone else, the lucky devil.

"OK, Annie. How can I help you today?"

Two days later, Annie and Sean were at Rosemont again with Sean's solicitor and Mary. Several police cars had arrived. Annie had brought along Jacqueline's old nanny Bridget, the elderly woman was filled with excitement at the prospect of seeing Jacqueline again.

Mary had made sure that Miss Pritchard knew nothing of their plans and the shocked expression on the woman's face when the police arrived was really something to behold. It made Mary feel that the miserable time she had spent at Rosemont had been truly worth it.

Annie asked to be the first to see her mother. She was nervous and hesitant as she made her way ahead of the rest of the group. Her mind was racing. What if her mother was beyond help? She pushed the negative thought away and continued down the long corridor.

The first thing she noticed was that the name on the door said Joan Taylor; her grandparents had placed Jacqueline in the hospital under a false name. Annie's hands were shaking as she unlocked the door and entered the room.

The woman in the room looked up in surprise. For the first time in twenty-five years Annie knew she was staring at her real mother. She moved slowly, so not to frighten her, and whispered: "Hello, I'm Annie."

Jacqueline was surprised to see a stranger in her room. She moved slowly to her bed and sat on the side holding onto her doll. Annie quietly sat down next to her.

Jacqueline looked at her and smiled.

"This is my baby. She's called Annie, she's my little girl."

Annie's eyes filled with tears as she watched her mother cuddle the old doll. She studied her mother. She looked older than her forty-one years and it was a crime the way they had chopped off all her pretty auburn hair.

Her head had been almost shaved; the hair was about half an inch long all over. They obviously hadn't been feeding her properly. She was just skin and bone. Her face was bloated and her skin had a yellow tinge, probably jaundiced from the medicines they were giving her to keep her quiet. She looked like someone from a wartime prison camp instead of a hospital.

Annie studied her closely. Was she drugged? What had they been giving her and was she addicted to the medicine?

She reached out and touched her mother's arm.

"My name is Annie as well. Would you like to go for a walk in the garden with me and see Bridget?"

At the mention of Bridget, Jacqueline's eyes lit up. She knew the name. Was her nanny really here? She studied the stranger. Was this new woman just like Miss Pritchard? Was she trying to confuse her so she could hurt her? She pulled away from Annie's hand.

"I don't like you," she said in a slurred voice. "You're trying to trick me. Miss Pritchard told me that Bridget was dead. You're trying to trick me so you can give me more medicine."

And with that she pushed her daughter hard.

Annie fell off the bed and landed on the floor with a loud thud. Jacqueline stared down at her and screamed: "I hate you. You're just like Miss Pritchard, trying to trick me. I'm not going to talk to you any more."

Bridget had been standing just outside the door and heard what was going on. She decided now was the time to intervene and entered the room with her arms open wide. Jacqueline felt panicked seeing the older woman. Had she done something wrong? Was someone else coming to hurt her?

Bridget moved slowly closer and pursed her lips.

"Now, Jackie, is that any way to behave? Look what you've done to the nice lady."

Jacqueline stared at her for what seemed like ages, then a light clicked in her drugged brain and she realized it really was Bridget, her old nanny.

Annie moved away to the other side of the room and watched her mother's face light up with happiness as she leapt into Bridget's arms. "Bridget, you're alive. Oh my God…she was right…the lady was right, you are still alive."

From her vantage point, Annie quietly bawled her eyes out as she watched her mother's reaction. There was such joy on her face as Jacqueline held Bridget in her arms and the love she felt for her nanny lit up her pasty face. The doll she had been hanging on to fell near Annie's feet. She gently picked it up.

The police had a lot of questions that needed answers from Miss Pritchard and she knew she was in big trouble and could possibly go to jail for a long time. She placed all the blame squarely on Edward Ryan's shoulders. He had shown her a letter from a doctor that said his daughter was a danger to herself. When the police asked if she had ever actually spoken to the doctor about her patient's care, Pritchard admitted she hadn't contacted him; she had never even met him. She only had Edward Ryan's word that the man existed.

Over the next few weeks, Annie bought a small house for her mother and Bridget at The Docklands, a new development on Dublin's waterfront. It had been the show house and was already fully furnished; it made things a lot easier for them.

Bridget was relieved to leave the Ryan household and moved in to help take care of Jacqueline, who she still looked upon as her own daughter.

The house had spectacular views of the waterfront and Annie stayed there with them three nights a week, spending the other nights with Sean at his home in Killiney. She was so in love with him that sometimes she was afraid of her own feelings. What if he left her, one day for someone else, as her father had done to Mary? Sean was usually on the road a lot, touring, and he met a lot of good-looking young women. She wanted desperately to let him get closer to her, but deep down she was still afraid of letting him into her heart.

Bridget needed help handling Jacqueline, who was not an easy patient. For twenty-five years she had been told what to do and when to do it, locked in that tiny room with just a bed, a small table and one chair. She found it hard to adjust to so much space. All the changes made her nervous, and when she was nervous she became fearful of everything. She would panic over the slightest change to her daily schedule or food. She still insisted on Bridget taking her to the bathroom, the way the nurse had done in the hospital. She expected the same food she had been given at the hospital. Preparing good, nutritious meals to gradually change her diet took all of Bridget's ingenuity and patience.

A doctor visited her twice a week, gradually weaning her off the cocktail of drugs she had been taking for most of her life. Physically she looked much better. Her skin had lost the jaundiced appearance and her eyes were no longer puffy. Working with her and convincing her to try something new was the hardest part; it was an almost impossible task.

There was the time Bridget and Annie took her for a walk along the waterfront. Jacqueline was so afraid of passers-by that she insisted on walking between the two of them. Bridget asked her what it was she was afraid of and she replied she was afraid the people had come to take her away. At times she acted like a spoilt child, throwing whatever she didn't like onto the floor. Many of their good dishes were smashed during that period and had to be quickly replaced.

When Annie felt angry with her mother, she forced herself to remember what the woman had been through.

One morning, Bridget had survived yet another temper tantrum. As she was cleaning-up the destruction Jacqueline had caused, she suggested counselling. Annie thought it was a good idea. She made several telephone calls and was referred to John Walsh, a well-known psychiatrist in Dublin. He suggested that the three of them should attend group therapy. He felt it would work best for Jacqueline, who would be too nervous to visit him alone.

The visits were a tremendous help for all three of them. Jacqueline benefited enormously and it helped Annie come to grips with the deep-seated issues she still had regarding her stepmother.

After about a dozen sessions, Jacqueline seemed to finally understand what had happened to her. At the end of four months she appeared to have more control over her temper and the bouts of depression were lessening. Their relationship was finally looking up. With the help of the doctor and the psychiatrist, Bridget was weaning her off the last of the drugs that had kept her a prisoner for so many years. It had been a slow process, but it was finally working.

It was February and the weather was bitterly cold outside. Jacqueline was in her pretty yellow bedroom with the white embroidery Anglicise curtains and matching bedspread. The room was so different than the small, grey hospital room she had lived in for so many years. She was lying on her big comfortable bed, pretending to be asleep.

She still felt bewildered, at times, by all the changes that had taken place in her life. She understood who Bridget was, but still couldn't understand who the other woman, called Annie, was, or why she was living with them. She liked her and knew she was always very kind.

But that day she looked at herself for several minutes in the big full-length mirror, and was shocked by what she saw. When she had been in the hospital, they wouldn't give her a mirror, so she had imagined she looked as she did at sixteen. Her face had been young and pretty then.

Tears filled her eyes; she suddenly remembered John. Where was he? Why hadn't he come to see her? What had happened to him and why had he let them put her in hospital? She panicked. Didn't he love her any more? Why had she been placed in that awful place? If only she could remember how she got there?

Why hadn't her mother and father stopped them from locking her up? Didn't they love her anymore or care what was happening to her? All these questions and thoughts rushed around in her head.

She remembered the pain of giving birth to John's child and knew she had called her Annie, after John's mother. It was the same name as the woman who lived with them. Maybe she was a relative. Jacqueline felt exhausted trying to sort out her thinking and, in minutes, she was fast asleep and dreaming of John.

It was a glorious day and she felt so happy. She was walking on top of the cliffs on Inish Mann with John and he had his arm around her waist. But when she turned around to kiss him, he was gone. In his place was a stranger who grabbed her and tried to kiss her; when she resisted he pushed her down on the ground and was on top of her.

She woke up screaming.

Bridget raced into the room and took her in her arms.

"There, there…it's alright my darling," she cooed, softly. "Bridget's here, I won't let anyone hurt you. You were having a bad dream."

As the weeks passed, Jacqueline improved physically, but mentally she was still unable to cope with life or the world around her. She insisted on leaving all the windows and door of her room open, making it difficult to keep the house warm during the winter weather outside. The wind and rain poured in, and they had to keep the heater on at full blast just to keep her room at a reasonable temperature.

Bridget and Annie tried to explain that, in bad weather, people usually closed their windows, but Jacqueline would have none of it. She did her best to explain to them what it had been like being confined in an enclosed space with the only light she saw coming through a small round piece of glass in the locked door. She couldn't bear the thought of feeling locked up again, having the windows and door closed.

A number of times Bridget found her sitting at the open bedroom window, watching the people go by in the street outside. It was as if she only wanted to observe what was happening in the world without actually becoming a part of it.

She had been told so many times she was mentally ill that she now believed it. Her excuse for not going out for a walk with Annie or Bridget was: "Oh, I couldn't. It's not safe, I'm mentally ill."

There were times when Annie almost gave up on her mother. Maybe Jacqueline had just been locked away too long. Maybe she would never be able to cope with the outside world. But, just as she was about to give up, Jacqueline would become totally logical and bring up something from her past.

One day she asked them at dinner: "Why didn't my mother come to the hospital to see me? Was she ashamed of me? Is that why she only came to see me once?"

Bridget eyes filled with tears.

"No, darlin', she wasn't ashamed of you. She just felt bad because she had left you there for such a long time when you should never have been there at all."

Jacqueline listened carefully to Bridget's explanation. She was taking it all in. Then she replied.

"But you don't understand, Bridget. My mother was right; I am mentally ill, Miss Pritchard told me so."

Annie reached for her mother's hand.

"No, that's not true. You're not mentally ill."

Jacqueline looked at Annie, then back at Bridget. Who should she believe? Miss Pritchard had said that she was mentally ill. She could be a danger to others.

Jacqueline took Bridget's hand.

"Miss Pritchard told me I was locked up because I had hurt someone. She said I was sick when I did it. I don't remember hurting anyone, so I must be mentally ill."

Annie was livid with Miss Pritchard. She would make sure the woman suffered for what she did and spend time in jail. The woman had used lies to brainwash Jacqueline. She had made her believe she was a menace to society by keeping her locked away. Bridget knew it was time to tell Jacqueline how many years she had spent at Rosemont hospital.

Jacqueline was stunned and rushed into her room, inconsolable with grief. Bridget left her alone for a few minutes before she went in and took her in her arms. She explained what she knew, but without saying that John was dead and Annie was her daughter.

Then, two weeks later, Jacqueline's memory started to return. At first, it was just little snippets of things, like remembering when she played tennis with John. When she asked why he hadn't been to see her, Bridget still didn't have the heart to say he was dead. What if she suffered a relapse? Somehow Bridget always managed to change the subject.

By the end of the next month Jacqueline was much improved. The good food, the love and attention, and the group therapy were beginning to pay off. Her face and body had lost their jaundiced appearance and had filled out. As if by magic, she was turning into an attractive middle-aged woman who resembled the daughter she didn't know about.

They all knew the metamorphosis was complete when, a week later, Annie returned from shopping with a number of pretty new outfits for her mother. And she had a massage therapist, a make-up artist and hairdresser with her. Some hours later, the experts had finished their work. Then Annie handed her mother, a cream-coloured twin-set, and a plum and cream-coloured tweed, straight skirt, along with two-tone cream and plum pumps to put on. After her mother was dressed, she led her to a full-length mirror and placed a string of pearls around her neck.

When Jacqueline saw her reflection in the mirror, she threw her arms around her daughter, and gave her a big hug. Annie's eyes filled with tears of joy as she studied the attractive woman in front of her. With Bridget's help and Annie's determination, they had accomplished a miracle. It had been a tough six months but finally there was light at the end of the tunnel. She was proud of Jacqueline and what the three of them had accomplished.

Two more weeks later, Jacqueline remembered nursing her baby girl. She wanted to know what had happened to her. Bridget carefully explained that the baby was now a grown woman and this time she did tell her Annie was her missing daughter.

At first, Jacqueline didn't want to believe her. How could Annie be her daughter? The last time she had seen the child she was just two years old. She studied Annie, who she thought was just a friend, and tried to picture her as the little girl she had loved with all her heart. She just couldn't make any sense of it.

She asked Annie to bring her photographs of when she was a child. Annie felt that before her mother saw anything she had to let her mother know that John had raised her and that he was now dead.

She had to prepare her mother carefully. He was in most of the photographs. She broke the news by explaining about the letter he had left for her when he died—and handed Jacqueline the letter, along with the photographs.

Jacqueline mourned John for over a week, refusing to leave her bedroom. It was the following Sunday before Bridget could coax her out of the room to join them. Now that her memory had begun to return, she wanted to know all about the years she had missed. Why had her father taken her daughter away and put her up for adoption? He had ruined all their lives. Through his actions Jacqueline had missed out on most of Annie's growing-up years.

Bridget went to her side and stroked her hand.

"There, there, me darlin', I know he was a dreadful man but, because of Annie, you've been given a second chance."

She sat down next to Jacqueline and elaborated.

"You have a wonderful daughter. She never gave up on finding you and now the two of you can make up for the all the time you missed. It's not healthy to keep looking back. Try to look forward to your future with Annie instead."

Jacqueline still couldn't let it go. She had one more question to ask. She studied the older woman's lined face.

"You were more like a mother to me and my brothers when we were growing up. How could you let my parents put me away? Why didn't you call the police when it happened? Why did you let them ruin my life?"

Bridget was hurt and taken aback by her questions and tears filled her eyes as she studied Jacqueline.

"Please forgive me. I believed your father when he said you had drowned. He even held a wake for you and invited all his business associates."

"And what about my mother?" pushed Jacqueline. "He must have told her I was alive and in Rosemont. How could she let him get away with it? How could she let her husband commit her daughter to a mental hospital when there was nothing wrong with her and then pretend she was dead?"

Bridget didn't want to hurt Jacqueline by telling her how selfish her mother was, but she had to let her know what had happened. She tried to soften the blow by explaining that Elizabeth was a career woman who worked ten hours a day and didn't have time to take care of her family. Elizabeth had hired Bridget as a nanny when she was in the latter stages of pregnancy, and when the twin boys were born they were handed over to Bridget. And it had been the same when Jacqueline was born. It was the way Elizabeth had been raised.

Bridget explained carefully that she herself had never married. Taking care of Jacqueline and her brothers had fulfilled her totally and she loved each one of them as if they were her own.

She didn't tell Jacqueline, that late at night, when her three little charges were fast asleep, she would look in on them and kiss them goodnight. Many a time she wondered why her employers didn't appreciate what little treasures they had.

The twins were carbon copies of each other, with their freckled pixie faces and bright red hair. They both loved adventure stories and many nights Bridget would find one or the other of them reading their favourite book under the covers with a torch. She hated chastising them but knew that if their mother caught them they would be in real trouble.

Jackie (she now called her that) was her favourite; she was a loner with her father's striking good looks. She was a real beauty with her large hazel eyes and auburn hair. She had been very athletic as a child and loved sports, especially tennis. She was such a bright little girl. Bridget told her about the day she had said that, when she grew up, she wanted to be the first lady barrister in her daddy's office. She was eight at the time.

The Jacqueline that Bridget knew then would never have allowed anyone to lock her up. They must have filled her full of drugs to keep her quiet. Being locked away for all those years had nearly broken her wonderful spirit.

CHAPTER 25

As promised, Annie brought the photograph album and the letter from her father for Jacqueline to see. The pictures held lots of memories, especially the ones with her father. She handed the album and letter to Jackie, who asked if she could look at the pictures alone. Annie said she understood and Jacqueline took them into her bedroom.

Bridget and Annie watched her as she closed the bedroom door firmly behind her without a backward glance. They smiled at each other. Closing that door signalled another breakthrough.

Jacqueline emerged later that day from the room and put the album on the kitchen table. She asked Annie to explain where each photograph had been taken, running her finger over each picture of John, as if touching his picture would bring him back.

Annie told her that he had never forgotten her and had always loved her. The reason he hadn't searched for her was because he had been told that she drowned along with Tim O'Shea. She never mentioned her father's fear of Edward Ryan.

Annie still felt ashamed of her father; feeling he was to blame for what had happened to her mother. If she had been him, she would never have rested until she had absolute proof of Jacqueline's death.

If her father hadn't been so easily bullied by her grandfather he would have searched for the woman he loved. She would never forgive him for not trying harder to find her. They had all suffered so much pain and loss because of his cowardice.

A few weeks later, Annie asked her mother if she would like to go with her on a business trip to London. She felt her mother was now ready to see a bit more of the world and she really had to see first-hand how her business was doing under Terri and Christian. Jackie's eyes sparkled with excitement at the idea of going away, but Bridget was worried about how she would fare without her.

Jackie could still be very petulant if she didn't get her own way. The childlike quality worried Bridget, but she knew that, if Jackie were to grow as a person, she had to let her make her own mistakes.

The day arrived and the two women left for Dublin Airport. In a couple of hours they were in London. Terri was there at Heathrow to meet them, grinning broadly. Annie couldn't help noticing how smart and business-like her friend looked. So much had happened to both of them during the previous few months. She had kept Terri up-to-date on what was going on and Terri was excited to finally meet Annie's mother.

As she studied Jackie, she was amazed at how well she looked. Annie had told her how it had been when they moved her out of Rosemont and she couldn't get over how well the woman looked. Anyone seeing Jacqueline, now, would think she didn't have a care in the world and had never suffered more than a broken fingernail. The woman was blessed with perfect features and a tall slim figure. The change was nothing short of a miracle. It was just another example of what love, patience and a determined woman like Annie could accomplish when she set her mind to it.

The three of them spent a wonderful day together. They shopped and lunched and just spent the whole time enjoying each other's company. Jacqueline was intrigued by the exciting city. She loved the variety of accents and dialects on the streets. It seemed that every nationality in the world was represented on that lovely, spring day as the three women walked arm-in-arm down Oxford Street.

They were all walked-out by the time they said goodbye to Terri on Welbeck Street. Annie and Jacqueline were staying at the Clifton Ford, a fairly small intimate hotel with a warm cosy atmosphere. Annie had stayed there many times in the past and most of the staff remembered her by name. As many of the staff were Irish, Annie felt her mother would feel right at home there.

She couldn't wait to introduce her mother to some of her friends. The first couple Annie invited to dinner included the person who had managed her career when she was modelling. Thelma was an attractive blonde woman who had always been there for Annie. She was happily married to Tom, a world-renowned doctor, who was a caring individual.

Annie had kept them up-to-date in the search for her mother. When she had thought her mother was dead, they had told her she shouldn't feel sad if things didn't work out. They were such kind, loving people. Annie couldn't wait to see their faces when they finally met Jacqueline.

When Annie and Jackie arrived at the restaurant in The Langham hotel, Tom and Thelma were already at the table enjoying a pre-dinner glass of wine. Annie spotted them before they saw her. As usual they were elegantly dressed and chatting away like newly-weds. Annie walked towards them holding her mother's hand. Always the gentleman, Tom stood up and greeted them and Annie noticed that his eyes never left Jacqueline's face.

Annie kissed them both and introduced her mother. Thelma hugged Jacqueline.

"You are just as lovely as your daughter," she said, smiling.

They had a wonderful evening together. At first Jacqueline felt shy but, after her first ever glass of wine, she began to unwind and enjoy herself.

They left the hotel restaurant and went to Thelma and Tom's house, a couple of streets away, talking and laughing into the wee small hours.

When they left and walked back towards their hotel, Annie told her mother how much they both owed Tom. When she was having problems with Jacqueline she had contacted him and explained how hopeless she felt. She explained to him that she felt her mother had become institutionalised and didn't know if she would ever be well enough to cope with the outside world.

Tom had told her to hang in there and not give up. He told her not to worry and was the one who had put them together with John Walsh, the doctor in Dublin. John had kept Tom in the picture, regarding Jacqueline's condition.

The following day Annie took Jacqueline to Harrods, London's biggest and most exciting department store. The range of things there overawed Jacqueline; it was filled with beautiful things from every country in the world. They spent the whole wonderful day together and literally shopped 'til they dropped. Jackie bought Bridget a lovely turquoise necklace as a souvenir of their trip.

The next day Annie had to work, so she had arranged to drop her mother off at one of the top spas. They were given instructions to give Jacqueline the works, massage, pedicure, facial and a manicure. She wanted to spoil her mother and a day at the spa seemed the perfect way to do it.

Annie told the receptionist to make sure her mother waited for her if they finished early and, satisfied with her reply, she left her mother at the spa and went to the office to meet with Terri and the rest of her staff.

The business meeting went well and it was decided that Terri would handle the London operation permanently. Chatting after the meeting was over, Annie had told Terri she was in love with Sean and was thinking of setting up a branch of the cosmetic business in Dublin, giving her more time to spend with him and her mother.

The meeting had taken longer than anticipated and she was running late. She grabbed the first taxi she could find to go directly to the spa and asked the driver to wait outside for her.

She went into the spa, and looked around the reception area for her mother. There was no sign of her. The receptionist she had spoken to earlier was no longer on duty and no one seemed to know anything. Annie raced through the spa looking for the girl she had spoken to earlier. She finally tracked her down in a back room having a smoke.

She screamed at the girl. "Where's my mother? I asked you to look after her and see she waited for me here!"

The girl glared back at her.

"How should *I* know where your mother is? She told me she was going back to her hotel. Why don't you look for her there?"

Annie was furious. She should report her to the boss, but that would take too much time. She hurried out of the door, into the waiting taxi and straight to their hotel. As soon as she had paid the driver, and the hotel doorman opened the heavy lobby door for her. She raced past him, praying silently that her mother would be there waiting. She was nowhere to be seen.

She panicked, asking the girl on reception if her mother had asked for a room key. No, both keys were still there.

Tables were set up for afternoon tea in the lobby and Annie collapsed, exhausted, into a chair. What should she do? Why hadn't she brought Bridget with her to look after her mother? Should she call the police?

Her mind was filled with all the terrible things that could have happened. Maybe her mother had been in an accident and was lying in a hospital somewhere. She should have taken her to the meeting with her. She should never have left her alone at the spa. Tears filled her eyes. If only Sean were here, he'd know what to do.

She was so lost in her thoughts that, for a moment, she didn't notice the handsomely dressed man in his forties, until he tapped her on the shoulder.

"I say," he said in a plumy British accent.

"This lady claims she's your mother. I find it hard to believe, she looks more like your sister to me."

Annie looked up at the man smiling down at her. Jacqueline was standing just behind him, giggling like a schoolgirl. Annie was astounded.

"I told you we'd find my Annie," Jacqueline said, touching his arm. She sounded so relaxed and happy.

"You see, Richard, I was right. I said this was my hotel."

The man smiled graciously back at her.

"You're right Jackie, but this is the *sixth* hotel we've tried."

Annie stood up and hugged her mother tightly, the anxiety draining away and relief now showing on her face.

"I was so worried," she said, releasing her. Then she remembered her manners.

"Please sit down and join us for tea and tell me where you found her."

She was pleased, but a teeny bit jealous that her mother had made a new friend. She realised she had no right to control Jacqueline's life. She was a woman and she needed a male friend as much as Annie did.

She studied this 'Richard' and her mother together. She noticed how happy her mother looked in his company and saw the way he smiled back at her. It was obvious he was attracted to her. She wondered if he was married and lived in London.

He explained that her mother had stopped him and asked for directions to her hotel, but had the wrong name; and when she seemed worried about finding the place, he had offered to help. He smiled at Annie.

"I'm really glad I was the one she asked. I've spent two wonderful hours with her."

Jacqueline was pleased with herself. She smiled and took his hand.

"Richard lives alone in London. His wife died five years ago, and he has a place in Ireland."

Annie couldn't help thinking how cold and uncaring her mother sounded when she spoke of Richard's dead wife. She knew she didn't mean it to sound that way, at heart her mother was still a child. There hadn't been time for her to grow up properly and learn the correct way of phrasing things. In her mind she was still sixteen. Annie put her arms around her and, like the child she still was, Jacqueline hugged her back.

"Don't you think it's nice, Annie?" she asked, in a breathless whisper that begged her daughter to like Richard.

"I mean, that Richard has a house in Ireland?"

Annie couldn't help smiling; Jacqueline sounded like a girl with her first crush.

"I think it's wonderful. Richard can come and visit us whenever he's there."

Richard got as far as "I have a house in Wicklow…" before Jacqueline cut in excitedly.

"He's promised to stop in and see us each time he visits Wicklow."

Richard smiled: "That is, if it's OK with your daughter? By the way my last name is Hewett."

Annie nodded and smiled back.

"We'd be delighted to see you. What do you do for a living?" she asked, as she handed him a business card with her telephone number.

"I'm a theatrical agent. I represent a number of actors and musicians in London—and in Ireland."

That evening they flew back to Ireland. Annie was anxious to see Sean. She had really missed him. She collected her rental car and dropped her mother off at the house with Bridget. Jacqueline couldn't wait to tell Bridget all about the trip and how she met Richard—and to give her the necklace she'd bought for her as a present.

As Annie left, her mother was positively glowing and she felt a little worried that Jackie might end up disappointed if the Richard thing didn't work out. She was like a teenager with a big crush.

She put her worries aside and headed for Sean's house. He'd been in Germany with the band and she had really missed him. He had cooked dinner for them; coquilles Saint-Jacque, and served it with a delightfully light French white wine. When dinner was over they sat in front of a roaring fire with their glasses of wine. The Brandenburg Concerto No.3 was playing softly in the background.

Sean listened to her stories of London and chuckled when he heard about her mother's adventure. He thought it was hilarious the way she had found an attractive man to chase all over London with until she finally found the right hotel.

"That's our girl," he chuckled. "She's a man magnet, just like her daughter!"

"Oh, so you think I'm a man magnet, do you?"

Annie giggled, setting her glass down and tickling him until he begged her to stop.

He threatened to tickle her back if she didn't stop and they toppled noisily off the sofa, tickling each other and screaming with laughter. He pinned her arms to her sides so she couldn't tickle him anymore and kissed her. She responded as he hoped she would and he felt a fire start in his belly, they both wanted each other. He undressed her, kissing each part of her body as he uncovered it. She was filled with love for him and responded with the same desperate need to make love. As their bodies came together it was as if they had become one entity.

Later that night Annie lay on the rug in front of the fire, relaxed and spent, enjoying the moment. Sean stood up naked and pretended to stagger as he made his way to the bedroom. Annie giggled. He was always clowning about. He returned a few moments later with a couple of large pillows and a comforter. He noticed she was studying his body and there was a smile on her face. It made him feel a little self-conscious and he covered his feelings—and other things—with a grin.

"I just hope you're not comparing me to all those gorgeous British blokes?"

She looked surprised.

"You know, all the gorgeous men I've seen you photographed with."

She giggled.

"Oh those. They were usually actors and models. The dates were set up by our agent to help our careers; most of them were gay with very nice boyfriends of their own."

That was the moment she realized how much he meant to her. He was the man she had been waiting for all her life. It seemed odd to think that he had been within her grasp all along.

He set the pillows down and lovingly covered her beautiful naked body with the comforter. He seemed nervous and ill-at-ease, though, and she wondered what was making him appear that way. What if he didn't feel the same about her, if he didn't love her as much as she loved him? She had to stop imagining things.

She looked into his eyes and recognized that it was going to be OK; he loved her. He bent towards her and took her left hand in his.

"Annie, will you marry me? I want you with me for the rest of my life, please say yes, say you'll marry me."

Annie had tears in her eyes before she could answer.

"Oh, Sean, yes…yes, I'd love to marry you."

He felt so happy that his face was beginning to hurt from grinning so much. He stood up and moved to the mantelpiece where he brought down a small, dark green velvet box. He opened it and removed an emerald and diamond ring from the dark velvet interior. Then he slipped the ring on her finger.

"And that makes it official," he said, smiling happily.

Later that evening they were discussing how soon they should tell their relatives and friends about their engagement, when the phone rang.

It was Bridget and she sounded anxious. She told Annie that Jacqueline's memory of the days immediately before she was placed in the hospital had returned. There was a problem. Could Annie and Sean come over right away?

They dressed quickly and drove into Dublin. They got to the house in record time and Bridget opened the door to them, tears running down her cheeks. Annie was very concerned as she approached her. Bridget was wearing her 'Super Chef' apron and used it to wipe away the tears. Her voice broke as she whispered croakily.

"Your grandfather killed a man in front of Jacqueline, that's the reason he had her locked away."

Sean looked confused.

"Who was it," he asked. "Whom did he kill?"

"It was Tim O'Shea, John's business partner," Bridget said.

"He saw Jacqueline and Tim board the ferry for Inish Mann and followed them to the island."

Annie sat on the sofa next to her mother. Jacqueline's eyes were red and swollen from crying. They hugged as she whispered: "I was right there; I watched my father kill Tim. It was really awful."

Annie took her hand and said softly.

"Try to remember everything that happened that day if you can?"

Jacqueline looked sad.

"Well, as you already know, Tim and I took the ferry from Galway to Inish Mann. John had sent Tim in his place because he was still married to Mary and was afraid of my father finding out."

Annie handed her mother a tissue and she wiped the tears from her eyes before she continued.

"The plan was that Tim would take me to John and we would pick you up from Bridget and escape to England with no one the wiser. As last we would be a family." She stifled another sob as she continued.

"Bridget was looking after you and I knew she would help us when the time came."

Her voice broke off and she hesitated remembering.

"It was a lovely summer day and, when we got to the island, Tim and I walked to the top of the cliffs to get a better view. I'd brought along some food for lunch and an old blanket for us to sit on."

She swallowed hard.

"I never expected what happened next. As I placed the blanket on the ground, Tim made a grab for me."

She paused, shivering as she relived what happened next.

"I was stunned. He had always been just a friend to me and he was John's business partner. I told him to stop and leave me alone, but he held me even tighter. I begged him to please let me go," she wiped a tear away.

"Then he told me that he had always loved me."

Her voice broke off, as if the memory of what had happened next was almost too painful to remember.

"I tried pushing him off me but he was very strong. I suppose there was no going back for him. He knew his actions had ruined his relationship with John, so he tried to make love to me. When he touched my breasts I screamed and that's when my father appeared. He hauled Tim off me."

She paused.

"At first I was glad to see Daddy and I told him Tim was just a friend. But he wouldn't listen to me. He called Tim terrible names and then he hit him."

Annie handed her a tissue to wipe her eyes as Jacqueline revealed more.

"Tim hit my father back as hard as he could. He was young and strong but was still no match for my father. I tried to separate them but they pushed me away and I must have hit my head on a stone and passed out. I remember coming to and seeing blood on Tim's head; he was unconscious and my father was dragging him to the edge of the cliff. Then I saw him throw his lifeless body over the edge."

The memory of what had happened that day was etched on Jacqueline's face. Tears ran down her cheeks as she whispered:

"I suppose I couldn't face what happened and had a nervous breakdown."

CHAPTER 26

Edward Ryan watched angrily as his wife stood by the front door giving final directions to the movers. They had already taken everything she wanted out of the house. Then she turned and gave him a sly smile.

"By the way, I've already sold the majority of my shares in the company. If you need to get in touch with me I'll be at our accountant's apartment."

Edward moved towards her, looking half-crazed, and screamed: "You bitch!"

He moved even closer.

"You thoughtless, cold-hearted bitch. Wait 'til your boyfriend gets a load of the real you."

Then, trying desperately to control his anger, he held open the front door and shoved her outside.

"Good riddance to bad rubbish."

And he slammed the door shut behind her.

He was alone when the detectives knocked on the front door. Annie had given them all the information regarding his crimes. He was arrested for Tim's murder and the false imprisonment of his daughter.

His granddaughter had arranged for Dermot Moore to be present at the Ryan house when the police arrived to arrest Edward Ryan.

Dermot was to have the exclusive story. Annie felt it was the least she could do for him after the way he'd been treated. The reporter watched with glee as Edward Ryan was handcuffed and dragged from his home, screaming obscenities at the police. They had made a terrible mistake and he would make them pay for it. Didn't they know who he was...? Didn't they know whom they were dealing with...?

The Irish police ignored the insults and threats and pushed him roughly into the police car, with Dermot following close behind soaking up his exclusive.

He sold the story to an international newspaper and, the following day, when the story broke, the press applauded Dermot for his unfailing efforts to find Jacqueline.

He was considered a hero, and he was booked to appear on radio and television programmes in Ireland and Europe to talk about it.

Public opinion turned rapidly against Edward Ryan, not because of the murder, but because of what he did to his teenage daughter. Elizabeth Ryan was included in the public's contempt too.

The story of Annie's desperate search for her real mother Jacqueline—and Dermot's part in finding her—made the public want to hear more and he found himself in great demand. Dermot accepted a top position with a major newspaper and was offered his own radio show.

Edward Ryan was not a happy prisoner. He had just spoken with Peter Jones, his solicitor, who told him he didn't have the time to represent him. He was leaving Ireland for an extended holiday and would be away for the best part of two months. Edward was livid. Over the years Peter had been given most of his criminal cases to work on, as Edward specialized in corporate law. In the process Edward had made him very wealthy and now, just when he really needed his help, Jones was suddenly leaving the country.

Edward knew the man was lying. He didn't want to help because public opinion had turned against him. Jones was terrified some of it might rub off on him. Talk about rats leaving a sinking ship.

Edward got the same story from the next four solicitors he contacted. They were sorry, they were just too busy, or they didn't have time to take on such a difficult case.

For the first time in his life, he felt as if he was totally alone. He felt like giving up. His so-called friends and acquaintances looked on him as a pariah. What if his sons felt the same way and wouldn't help him because of what he did to their sister?

The police had shown him the photographs of his daughter; she looked really dreadful, like someone who had just been released from a concentration camp at the end of the war. That bloody woman, Pritchard, she had promised him she would take good care of his daughter. God knows he had paid her enough money.

He knew it was his own entire fault; everything had gotten out of control that day on the island when he lost his temper. If only he had handled things differently, controlled his temper, this would never have happened to Jacqueline. He should have checked up on his daughter, when she was at Rosemont and made sure she was being treated well. If only he had done things differently.

The next few days dragged by with Edward suffering untold fears of what the future held in store for him, as he waited for his sons to show up, and apply for his bail. He was not treated well as he languished in the holding cell. The room was filthy, with disgusting words written on the walls by previous prisoners, using their own excrement.

The cell held a single bed with a black rubber mattress and one thin blanket for warmth. There was a toilet without a seat, in one corner. He had no privacy and was checked every hour through the small glass window in the door of the cell. It was obvious to Ryan that the guard in charge hated his guts. And he was right. Gerald McCall had no time for him. If he was honest, he *really* hated the man. He had a long memory when it came to Ryan and the contempt he had shown towards his fellow officers.

The barrister had found immense fun in the courtroom by treating the police like fools. It was as if he had a vendetta against the men and women who worked to keep the criminals, often Ryan's own clients, off the streets. He didn't give a damn about the victims his clients had butchered or kneecapped. All he cared about was the dirty money he earned keeping the perpetrators out of jail. As far as Gerald McCall was concerned, Edward Ryan had grown rich on the blood of innocent people. Now it was payback time.

Edward had never felt so alone or afraid. It had been a shock when his wife left him. Deep down he knew she was having an affair, but it really hurt when he found it was with his own accountant. Elizabeth was just as bad as he was. He had never heard her ask to see Jacqueline. She was always too busy to visit their daughter at the hospital.

Edward still felt guilty about what had happened that awful day on Inish Mann. He remembered how incensed he felt when he saw the young man on top of Jacqueline. If only he had held his temper none of this would have happened. Instead, he beat the man senseless and his daughter was injured when she tried to separate them.

He hadn't meant to kill the young man but, when he did, he had compounded his crime by throwing the man's body over the cliff while his daughter looked on.

Edward would never forget the look of fear in Jacqueline's eyes and her terrified screams as he moved towards her. His actions had driven his daughter out of her mind.

He hadn't meant to hurt her, he had only wanted to stop the bleeding from the cut on the side of her head, but she wouldn't stop screaming…he had to do something.

He shivered, thinking someone had walked over his grave. He felt helpless and so alone. Was this how Jackie had felt at Rosemont? He hated himself for what he'd done to her. When had he turned into a monster?

As a young man he had worked his way through law school and his plans upon graduation were to represent the poor and downtrodden against the rich. That was before he met Elizabeth.

They met at her engagement party. Edward had been practising law for about a year when Tom McBride, an old classmate, invited him to his engagement party. Tom was not the brightest brain in Ireland and had only passed the Bar after four tries. But he was a nice enough bloke, even though he was born with a silver spoon in his mouth. As soon as he finished law school Tom joined his father's law firm; Edward doubted if anyone else would have hired him.

He remembered that he'd found the party extremely dull, with all those stuck-up society folks trying their one-up-man-ship on each other. A number of the married women had also made a play for him. He was about to leave when Elizabeth showed up.

There had been a virtual hush as the young woman entered the room. She was by far the most beautiful girl there and she knew it. She wore a sexy low-cut red dress with a slit up the side that reached the top of her thigh. She greeted Tom with a perfunctory kiss, while flirting with Edward over his shoulder.

Edward realised then that she was a tease and guessed that, by the end of the evening, he would get to sample the goods. Later that evening they wandered into the garden together, the party was in full swing, and by the cover of a large oak tree he removed her dress. She was naked underneath and that excited him all the more. He had taken her roughly and she enjoyed every minute of it. Their lovemaking had always been passionate and exciting. It was usually earth shattering for both of them.

Elizabeth was used to making love to timid, rich guys and was shocked by the excitement she experienced when she was around Edward. She couldn't keep her hands off him; she enjoyed a bit of rough and he gave her what she wanted.

He knew that, money-wise, he wasn't in her league, but he made a play for her anyway. He had gone after her, even though he knew she was engaged to his friend. In a way, knowing she was spoken for made the chase all the more exciting. And his persistence had paid off.

She fell in love with him and his friend never forgave him for stealing her away. Later on, Tom, married a nice gentle girl like himself, but he never forgave Edward. If he only knew what she was really like, he'd have thanked him for taking her off his hands.

Their problems started soon after they were married, when her family refused to accept him, treating him as though he was dirt. Her parents were stuck-up old bastards who thought they were better than everyone else.

Elizabeth was as just as bad as her parents. When he did something she didn't like, she would remind him that, without her and her family's money, he would have nothing. She didn't seem to understand that Edward was the one who had saved her father's firm from going under.

By the time he joined the business, her father had systematically run the business into the ground, with his old-fashioned management style. The man was still living on his past glories. Edward buckled down and made it his business to save the company. He had a talent for marketing and used every contact he had to make it a success.

Eventually he made them all a truck-load of money. But, somewhere along the line, he had lost himself and sold his immortal soul to the Devil.

Elizabeth hated Edward's family and, when she was around them, she acted as if they were inferior to her. She refused to let the kids visit them. His brothers and sisters had been terribly hurt by her actions. Why had he allowed his wife to have so much control over his life and the lives of their children? Was fame and fortune really more important to him than his own family?

Tears filled his eyes as he thought about Jacqueline. He had destroyed his beautiful daughter. At the time, it had been a judgement call; it was her life or his. If he confessed what had happened to Tim O'Shea, he would most definitely have ended up in prison and Jacqueline would have been off to England with her lover and their baby. He couldn't allow that to happen.

John O'Hanlon was not only years older than her, he was also a rogue. When Edward had had him checked out, he found out that Jacqueline was not the only woman he'd had affairs with. No way would he allow his daughter to end up with that womanising bastard.

If only he had checked out Miss Pritchard as thoroughly as he checked out O'Hanlon. If only he had gone to see his daughter on a regular basis. He would have known how Pritchard was treating her.

Jacqueline had been his favourite. She had a stubborn streak in her, just like her father, and was ambitious like him. When they played tennis, she did her best to beat him. He loved that about her. She was smart and her goal was to attend law school; she used to tell him that one-day she would become a barrister just like him. She loved hearing about cases and how he went about defending his clients.

All of that changed when she met O'Hanlon. He had also been part of ruining her life—getting her pregnant at sixteen. Even then Edward had hoped that things would work out. He made a pact with Jacqueline; she could keep the baby if she stayed away from her lover. Everything was working OK, until that slimy bastard O'Hanlon talked her into running away with him to England.

Then that awful wife of his contacted Edward and told him what was happening; if only he hadn't listened. He had followed Jacqueline to the Island…and the rest was history.

When he placed his daughter in Rosemont, he felt as if a part of him died. He honestly thought he was doing the right thing for her. She had suffered a breakdown. Why did he believe Ms Pritchard when she wrote to him saying that Jacqueline needed constant supervision? Why didn't he check things out for himself? He should have gone there and seen for himself. But he couldn't; he felt too guilty, having his daughter locked away.

His sin was not in killing Tim O'Shea, but in his cowardly treatment of his only daughter. One day he would have to meet his maker. How would he explain away what he did? How would he make amends? He couldn't…

The only person who visited him in prison was Kathy. She told him she had contacted his sons and they were on their way. At first they hadn't wanted to help him because of what he did to their sister. But she had talked them into at least seeing him.

Tears of relief filled Edward's eyes as he studied her pretty, smiling face. She was the only woman, besides his mother, who had ever tried to help him. Why hadn't he married a woman like her? He supposed it was because she had been his childhood friend; he had always thought of her more like a sister than a lover.

He studied her lovingly. The years had been kind to her. Kathy was one of those rare women who had grown more beautiful with age. She started her own management placement company, after her husband died. She dressed in a way that complimented her slim hips and full-breasted figure. He didn't feel anything brotherly about her now. He wanted to take her in his arms and kiss her soft pink lips. He felt so thankful to her.

He could trust her and she wanted to help him; he finally had someone he could trust in his corner, and maybe, just maybe, she could help him stay out of prison.

CHAPTER 27

Two weeks later, Mary answered the door to a man who asked if Annie O'Hanlon was there.

"Yes," Mary replied, eyeing him suspiciously. "What do you want with her?"

Annie heard the man ask for her and was curious, so she joined her stepmother on the doorstep. The man asked her if she was Annie O'Hanlon and, when she nodded, he handed her an envelope.

It was a notice to appear in court in two weeks. Her grandfather was suing her and Jacqueline for false arrest. The documents stated that Ryan had placed his daughter in Rosemont to prevent her from going to prison. He claimed she was the one who killed Tim O'Shea and that she had subsequently suffered a breakdown through the guilt she felt over his death. Whatever he did was done out of love, wanting to protect his only daughter.

Annie found it hard to believe that he would twist the truth by putting the blame for his actions on the daughter he had almost destroyed. She drove to Killiney to show Sean the subpoena and, when he read the document, he pointed out how essential it was that they find more proof against Edward Ryan.

At present, he had more going for him than they did. He was a well-known barrister who had represented a number of major clients. Some of them were known criminals, but others were judges and politicians who he had kept out of prison. Ryan would see that they paid him back in full. He knew powerful people in high places.

There was a good chance that the court would believe his story over Jacqueline's. Could she handle the pressure of a major court case? There was the chance that she might be looked on as mentally ill and not capable of telling the truth. At best her memory was still sketchy with regard to the murder.

Annie listened quietly to Sean's arguments and knew he was right. It would be months before her mother was well enough to face going into a courtroom. If she were forced to get up in court right now she might suffer another breakdown. They had to stall the proceedings long enough to collect enough evidence to prove Jacqueline's innocence.

Dermot Moore studied his new office with affection. Things had changed dramatically for him since his exclusive articles had appeared in the newspapers. He now had a top position with *The Star* and his very own secretary. He had no intention of losing what he had accomplished because of a lying bastard like Edward Ryan. He, too, had been visited by a process server that morning and was due to appear in court.

He wondered why Elizabeth Ryan was no longer part of the lawsuit. The million dollar question was, where was she hiding and how could he find her? He would have to do some major research to find out what was going on. He knew 'Ryan and Ryan' had changed hands, but who had sold it? Was it Edward, or was it Elizabeth? He would not allow them to get away with murder and the pain and suffering they had caused their only daughter.

He asked himself for the hundredth time why Elizabeth Ryan had taken off for places unknown right after she had visited her daughter in Rosemont. Had she finally discovered that she had a conscience? The staff at Rosemont told him it had been her only visit to the hospital in twenty-five years.

It was later that day that Dermot finished his research. He called Annie to let her know what he had found. As he dialled her number, he felt sure that Elizabeth was the key to unlocking the secret. He had to find out what she knew about the day Tim died.

Mary had just surprised Annie and Sean by admitting she was the one who had contacted Jacqueline's parents when John said he was leaving her for good and going with Jacqueline to England. It was also she who had discovered the rendezvous with Tim O'Shea and it was through her that Edward Ryan had followed his daughter to the Aran Isles.

Sean watched Annie fall apart in front of his eyes. He reached across the table and took her hand, trying to comfort her. As Mary explained the events, he watched the life leave the face of the woman he loved more than his own life. Annie had gasped as though in physical pain as she heard the part Mary had played in her mother's incarceration. Tears streamed down her cheeks as she studied her stepmother.

"How could you do it? And to think Daddy went to his grave not knowing why she hadn't shown up that night."

Mary slumped down in her chair looking lost. Her voice was a hoarse whisper as she replied.

"I had no idea what would happen when I got her parents involved. I loved your father with all my heart; I was his wife and I was willing to do anything to keep him. I couldn't let him leave me for a young girl," she sobbed.

"I've lived with this guilt for so many years. I only admitted it now because I thought it might help you to fight the case against your grandfather if I told you about it."

Mary was sorry she brought up the subject. Had she destroyed her relationship with Annie by trying to help?

"Surely you can find it in your heart to forgive me, Annie? Remember, I was the one who helped find Jacqueline. I know how much you love Sean. What would you do if some young girl tried to take him away from you?"

The phone rang and Annie picked it up, relieved that she didn't have to answer Mary's question. Dermot was on the line with news about her grandmother.

"Can we meet?"

"Yes," said Annie, before replacing the phone in its cradle. Her eyes met Sean's.

"That was Dermot, he has some news. We are to meet him at the pub in thirty minutes."

She was relieved that they had an excuse to leave. She didn't have to continue the conversation with her stepmother. She didn't know if she would be able to forgive her for what she had done to her mother.

Anxious to hear what Dermot had to tell them, they arrived at the pub ten minutes early and waited impatiently. They were both too shocked by Mary's latest revelation to say much. They sat at their usual corner table and waited.

In came a very different Dermot than the old one. Annie studied him, delighted with the changes. He wore a cream silk shirt and stylish black linen trousers. The shirt was on the long side, camouflaging his still-bulky waistline. Gone were the thin wispy strands of hair that had been so unattractive; his head was now shaved and she noticed a gold earring in one ear.

Annie felt the new look gave him an air of self-assurance; he looked like a man to be reckoned with.

"You look great, Dermot," she said, shaking his hand.

He blushed.

"I decided it was time I changed my image."

He sat erect and confident, facing them.

"Now for my news about Elizabeth. She's the one who took over the firm with her accountant. By the way, he's also her lover. I know that she plans on being in Dublin tomorrow to attend a business meeting. She expects to sell the remainder of her shares to a wealthy American."

"Do you know where she's staying?" Annie queried.

Dermot looked pleased with himself.

"She's already checked into The Four Seasons. We can have her subpoenaed and force her to answer questions about her daughter, and what happened the day Tim was killed, in court—that is, if we can get to her first.

"Why don't you let me take care of it; let me serve her the subpoena?" he added, with a big smile. "It would do my heart good!"

CHAPTER 28

It was six the next morning as Jacqueline closed the front door softly behind her. She didn't want to wake Bridget; she was afraid her elderly friend would not be happy with what she had in mind. Bridget wouldn't understand and would try to stop her from going to see her father.

Richard had agreed to help her. He was on a two- week visit to Ireland. She liked to think it was mainly because she was here. They had spent the past week together and she had enjoyed every minute of it. He was such a lovely man.

Now he was taking her to see her father. He understood that it was something she had to do. She hadn't been able to sleep the night before as she did her best to remember exactly what had happened to Tim. She was sure she hadn't killed him, but why was her father saying she did? Was it possible to kill someone and not remember it? She had to see her father and learn the truth.

As Richard drove towards Galway it brought back memories of the areas she used to frequent as a child. The picnics with Bridget and her brothers, it was strange that none of her childhood memories included her mother. On the other hand she had some joyful memories of moments spent with her father as a child. She had always felt he understood her and loved her, until that awful day on Inish Mann.

Richard glanced over at the pretty woman by his side. She meant everything to him. He hadn't felt like this about a woman since his wife was alive. Jacqueline had gone very quiet. He prayed that the visit to see her father wouldn't harm her mentally. Annie had told him what Jacqueline had gone through at 'Rosemont'. Maybe he should have checked it out with her first. He prayed that he was doing the right thing.

When they finally arrived at the Curragh Prison, Jacqueline sat for a couple of minutes in the car holding onto Richard's hand. He turned to her.

"Darling, are you really sure you are up to this?"

She nodded. Why was she so afraid to face her father? She must be strong she had to do this for Annie. She must be brave like her daughter and make things right.

It was time to take back control of her life and act like a woman. As she got out of the car she told Richard she would be back soon and with her head held high, she marched towards the prison gates.

As she went inside, she noticed there were three gardai (Policemen), on duty. They smiled at her, admiring the beautiful redheaded woman. One of them asked her what she wanted. She explained that she had come to see her father, Edward Ryan.

He looked surprised, gave her a long look and asked to search her bag. She wondered if he thought she might have a big file inside.

Minutes later she was ushered into Edward Ryan's cell. She was shocked to see her father. Sitting on his narrow bed he looked like a dejected old man. Surely this old man couldn't be her handsome father. He was in his early forties the last time she saw him.

She stood directly in front of him, gazing at him. What had she been so afraid of? He was nothing to fear, just a broken old man. She was the one who had been damaged. She hated him for what he did to her, he had ruined her life. He had taken everything from her. She had missed out on her daughter's childhood because of him. She felt such hatred towards him, she couldn't speak for what seemed ages. Then she said,

"In case you've forgotten me, I'm your daughter. You put me in Rosemont and forgot about me for twenty five years."

She saw the pain her words caused him and she enjoyed it. Let him suffer the way he had made her suffer. She watched as tears filled his eyes and as she continued her voice softened slightly.

"I've come to have a talk with you."

Edward's face lit up as he gazed at her in surprise. Could this really be Jacqueline, his only daughter? She looked lovely if a good deal older then when he had last seen her. He felt his spirit lift as he studied her.

She was healthy again. Thank God she didn't look anything like those awful pictures the media had printed of her when she was first released from Rosemont. She was going to be OK; he wanted to get down on his knees and thank God for this miracle.

He reached for her hand and she moved away slightly. Then she grasped that he didn't want to hurt her. Bravely, she faced him. He would never know how much courage it took for her to take his hand and sit down next to him.

He put his arms around her and held her to him, tears pouring down his face. She wiped the tears away with a white lace handkerchief.

"Now…," she said. "Let's talk about what really happened to Tim O'Shea."

CHAPTER 29

Elizabeth was taking a relaxing soak in the bathtub at the Four Seasons hotel. In four hours she was scheduled to fly to her villa in Cannes, where a new lover was waiting for her. He was thirty years younger than her and probably after her money; but, what the hell; no one knew her in France and she was having fun for the first time in years.

She had already dumped James, shortly after he set up the sale of her company. What a joke; he actually thought she would consider marrying him. She had just got rid of one bully. Why would she want to marry another one? She didn't need yet another man telling her what to do.

She knew that James loved to gamble while she did not. She liked a sure thing and had no intention of letting him throw away her money on the horses or at the track.

He had been well paid for his sexual services and made a lot of commission from the sale of her stock. She didn't owe him a thing.

As she lay there, enjoying the steamy hot water, she wondered what Edward would be like when he came out of prison. He had always been a domineering bully. Maybe jail would mellow him, but she doubted it. A leopard doesn't changes its spots.

She blamed him for everything. He was the one who had driven their sons away. He was difficult to get along with and had achieved so much in his law practice that the boys worried they wouldn't ever be able to live up to him. The very day they graduated from law school they left for England.

They had worked for a well-known firm in London before setting up their own business with money from the trust fund their grandparents had left them.

Although she had no feelings now for Edward, she did admire the way their sons had acted when they heard he was in trouble. They researched the evidence against him and suggested he should accept the lesser charge of manslaughter that was on offer from the prosecution. It was good advice and saved the family a lot of humiliation, as well as a drawn-out court battle and a great deal of ghastly publicity from news reporters and broadcasters.

Although Elizabeth was proud of her sons, she had never had much time for children, period. She hadn't wanted them when she married Edward—it had been his idea. He had been desperate for a son. Wouldn't you know that she'd find out too late that twins ran in both of their families? Thank God she'd had Bridget when they were born. She would have gone out of her mind without her help.

Bridget was sixteen when she started working for Elizabeth's parents. She had taken care of Elizabeth until she turned eight and was sent away to boarding school, and was then kept on as their housekeeper. After Elizabeth married and had the twins, Bridget moved in with her to help care for them. Her parents weren't happy about losing the woman, but they adored their grandsons and were willing to help.

Bridget was a natural and had loved the children as if they were her own. It had helped Elizabeth to regain her freedom—and her figure.

Ten years later Elizabeth gave birth to Jacqueline and, once again, Bridget took over the daily chores of raising a new baby.

Elizabeth made no excuse to anyone for the way she raised her children. Bridget was a very loving substitute mother and took excellent care of the three of them. Why was it that, if a man didn't bother with his children it was considered OK, but when a woman didn't have maternal feelings she was crucified by society?

Now the newspapers were having a field day with her reputation, calling her a cold-hearted bitch. They claimed she cared nothing for her children and had destroyed her daughter's life.

And, in order to save her own arse, that bloody woman Miss Pritchard had told them that Elizabeth hadn't bothered to visit her daughter in twenty-five years. The reporters didn't bother to ask her why she hadn't gone there. If they had, she would have told them she couldn't bear the idea of her daughter being defective or mentally ill.

The media had damaged her personal life and now Edward had managed to destroy the rest of her social standing in the community as well. She was glad to be leaving Ireland for good.

She hated Edward for the pain and disgrace he had put her through and for the embarrassment he had caused her family. The only thing she felt sad about was that he would probably only serve four years in prison.

Unbelievably it had been her testimony and Jacqueline's that had helped him prove his innocence. Under oath, Elizabeth was asked if she knew anything about the day Tim O'Shea was killed. She had to tell the truth. She had simply believed what Edward had told her the day he had Jacqueline incarcerated.

He had said a fight ensued when Edward found Tim O'Shea trying to rape his daughter. During the fight the younger man died and Edward had panicked. He had checked the man's pulse to make sure he was really dead before he tossed him over the side of the cliff.

Jacqueline substantiated her mother's story, telling the court that her father hadn't meant to kill Tim O'Shea, that it had been an accident. She stressed that she didn't want to press charges against him for locking her away in the Rosemont Clinic.

Elizabeth would never be able to understand her daughter. Why did Jacqueline feel she had to help her father after what he had done to her and the lies he made up about her, saying that she was the one who killed Tim O'Shea? If she had been in Jacqueline's shoes, she would have hung him out to dry.

She still had her doubts about the man's death being an accident. Then again, she supposed she was as much to blame as Edward was. If only she hadn't been so involved with business. She really should have checked out his story and made sure he had been telling the truth when he said that Jacqueline was mentally ill.

She had to let it go, she was giving herself a headache. She refused to be held responsible for what had happened. It was all Edward's fault; he was the one to blame. He had destroyed their lives and his mistakes had cost her a lot of money.

The judge charged both of them with Jacqueline's incarceration and they had to pay their daughter two million euros for the years she had lost. The lawsuit cost Elizabeth a million euros, plus another 500,000 in court costs. She didn't regret paying her daughter the money; she had already planned to set up a trust fund in her name.

It was the way the newspapers made her look. What really hurt was them saying she was a heartless, cruel woman. It was Edward who had ruined their lives, not her. She hated him with a passion.

A month later, Annie contacted Mary and invited her to afternoon tea at The Gresham, on the following Thursday at four o'clock. Mary was relieved and delighted to hear from her stepdaughter and made a point of arriving fifteen minutes early on the day in question.

Mary felt very nervous and wanted to get there before Annie to have time to think. She found a nice table facing the main doors and ordered tea and a scone from the waiter.

She knew she was being silly but had to know if Annie had forgiven her or still hated her. She would never forget the shocked look on her stepdaughter's face when she heard what she had done to Jacqueline.

She had spent the last few weeks praying Annie would forgive her for what she did. For twenty-five years Mary had told herself that she only did what any woman in love would do. Like Jacqueline, she too had suffered a loss, the loss of love and affection of the only man she had ever loved. Her husband had never been the same towards her after he met Jacqueline, and when he thought the girl had died he turned her memory into a shrine. She became the love of his life instead of what she really was, just another young girl he'd had a fling with. If she had known that he was a womaniser when he wanted to leave her for Jacqueline, she would have let him go. She believed the Jacqueline business had taken place because they had been separated at the time, but that was not the case.

She found out later that he had been involved with a number of other young women after Jacqueline. Somehow she had managed to look the other way and eventually he became too old or tired to attract them and settled down to life with her. She had always felt second best with him.

Annie adored her father and Mary didn't want to destroy the feelings she had for him, so she never told her about the other women. Annie still believed Jacqueline had been the only one.

Why did she feel so guilty, as if she were to blame for his carousing? What was it about young girls that fascinated him? She was only twenty-six when they were married. Why hadn't she been young enough for him?

Maybe his attraction to young girls had something to do with his childhood. She remembered her husband's mother, a strong-willed Kerry woman. John told her that his mother was in her mid-fifties when he was born. He didn't remember his father; he had died when he was two.

Mary hadn't got along well with John's mother. She was a bossy, controlling old woman with a will of iron, who hated her for taking her son away from her. The woman lived well into her nineties. Was she the reason her husband had favoured young girls?

Was he afraid to get involved with a mature woman because a mature woman would remind him of his mother? Was that why he picked young girls to have affairs with instead of grown-up women?

Mary sighed. She really didn't care about all this anymore. She had grown up during the past month and was now at a time in her life where it really didn't matter what her husband had done in the past; he couldn't hurt her anymore. It was time to forget him and begin living her life again.

And Armand, her lovely new French man friend, was just what she needed to forget John and the past. He had already visited Ireland a couple of times, since Paris, and they had gone out. There was a real attraction between them.

She had a good feeling about him; he treated her like a real woman. When they were together he didn't scan the room for something better the way John used to.

Up to now they had spent two weeks together and their relationship had grown stronger with each day. French men appreciated older women. She had heard they looked on women the way they did fine wine, as it ages it gets better and better.

Mary watched Annie enter the hotel lobby with Jacqueline. The two women walked in arm-in-arm and Mary felt a bit jealous. Annie spotted her and smiled, and she waved back feeling relieved. It was going to be OK.

She studied them as they headed towards her. Annie had worked hard to turn Jacqueline into a new woman, you could tell just by looking at her. She was totally different to the person Mary had first seen that day in the hospital ward.

With Annie and Bridget's help Jacqueline had changed radically. She looked years younger than Mary remembered. She was dressed in a soft pink tweed jacket and a matching short biased skirt; and with her new clothes and makeup she didn't look much older than her daughter. Her copper-coloured hair had grown back and had been cut to frame her face like a shining copper cap. Her eyes were made up in the latest style and her full mouth was now a soft shade of pink. As Mary studied the woman, she could understand what it was that had enticed her husband. No wonder he had wanted her.

When Annie and Jacqueline were seated at the table Mary noticed that three men sitting at the table nearby couldn't take their eyes off them. She smiled to herself. It was obvious that Annie was thrilled with what she had achieved with her mother and it was wonderful to see the way the two of them fitted together. They looked more like sisters than mother and daughter.

Mary didn't want to, but she still felt just the tiniest bit jealous as she watched them.

A young waiter moved to Jacqueline's side and leaned towards her with his pencil and order pad…and a flirtatious smile.

"And what can I get you, love?"

Annie and Jacqueline ordered tea and scones and he hurried away still smiling to himself. Then Annie spoke.

"I wanted to meet you here, Mammy, to give you the latest news on the court case."

Mary's eyes filled with happy tears. Annie had called her Mammy! She reached over the table to her and squeezed her hand.

"I love you Annie," she said softly.

"I know you do, Mammy. Jackie and I had a long talk last night and she feels like me, that you are my real mother. You raised me and took care of me. Jackie and I will always be very close but she can never replace you as my mother. That position is already taken."

Tears of happiness filled Mary's eyes as she listened.

"The case against my grandfather is over. He's going to spend four years in prison. Jackie helped save him from a much longer sentence. And the judge insisted my grandfather and grandmother pay her one million euros each for keeping her at Rosemont against her will."

Annie smiled at Jacqueline as she continued her explanation.

"I was so proud of you. I still can't believe that you went to the prison to talk with grandfather and sort him out. She smiled as she elaborated.

"And you held up so well when you gave your evidence."

Then she turned to Mary.

"The judge was impressed, and a little in love with her, by the time she'd finished."

Jacqueline smiled shyly.

"She's making that part up!"

Then she turned to Annie.

"You, my darling, were my rock. I couldn't have faced it without you."

Annie looked pleased.

"I'm just so happy that the trial's over. It solved a lot of problems and got rid of a lot of pressure and bad feelings."

She turned to Mary.

"And now, for the most important news of all. Sean has asked me to marry him and I've said yes!"

Mary threw her arms around Annie, thrilled by the news. She had always liked Sean; he was a good man and she knew he'd be faithful to her daughter. He wasn't the type to play around. He had spent a lot of time at her house when the band was at home in Ireland, running through new songs with her son and the other guys in the band. He was perfect for her daughter; she couldn't have picked a better man.

Annie smiled at her mother and stepmother.

"I'm going to need both of you to help me put my wedding together."

"Where will you live when you are married?" Mary asked, anxiously. "Will you be moving back to England?"

"NO," Annie replied firmly. "I'm staying right here in Ireland. I've made Terri my business partner because she did such a great job with the British side of my company. She not only held the company together while I was away, she made a good profit for us as well."

She smiled at them, looking contented.

"Oh, by the way, she just got engaged. She's going to marry Christian, my director, so I know that side of the business is in good order."

Then she studied the two women sitting facing her. They meant everything in the world to her. She was luckier than most people...she had two wonderful mothers. She smiled and reached for their hands.

"How would you both like to join me when I set up the Irish branch of my cosmetics company?"

They both nodded. Neither of them had any idea what it would involve, but they looked jubilant and gave her a resounding..."Yes!"

CPSIA information can be obtained at www.ICGtesting.com
Printed in the USA
BVOW07s1044211014

371687BV00001B/83/P

9 781424 155682